Down the Road to Eternity

DOWN THE ROAD TO ETERNITY
New and Selected Fiction

M.A.C. FARRANT

TALONBOOKS

Talonbooks
P.O. Box 2076, Vancouver, British Columbia, Canada V6B 3S3
www.talonbooks.com

Typeset in Adobe Garamond and printed and bound in Canada.
Printed on 30% post-industrial recycled paper.

First Printing: 2009

The publisher gratefully acknowledges the financial support of the Canada Council
for the Arts; the Government of Canada through the Book Publishing Industry
Development Program; and the Province of British Columbia through the British
Columbia Arts Council and the Book Publishing Tax Credit for our publishing
activities.

LIBRARY AND ARCHIVES CANADA CATALOGUING IN PUBLICATION

Farrant, M. A. C. (Marion Alice Coburn), 1947–
    Down the road to eternity : new & selected fiction / M.A.C. Farrant.

ISBN 978-0-88922-615-9

    I. Title.

PS8561.A76D69 2009   C813'.54   C2009-902843-3

Acknowledgements

Selections are from the following books:

Sick Pigeon (1991), Thistledown Press
Raw Material (1993), Arsenal Pulp Press
Altered Statements (1995), Arsenal Pulp Press
Word of Mouth (1996), Thistledown Press
What's True, Darling (1997), Polestar Press/Raincoast Publishing
Darwin Alone in the Universe (2003), Talonbooks
The Breakdown So Far (2007), Talonbooks

The quote used on page 264 is from "Essay on Gaming," *Harper's Magazine*, July 2008.

Cover painting, *Snow Owl Parking Meter*, by Gertrude Pacific of Sechelt, B.C., used with permission and thanks.

Special thanks to Karl Siegler for his help in choosing the selections, and for his thoughtful editorial advice.

Contents

In memory of my father,
Capt. W.D. (Billy) Gibson,
and for Terry

Foreword

Off Shore Navigation

Night and the order is given. You take your place at the wheel and pull away from the dock. How well you steer the ship around obstacles, knowing just where to manoeuvre past the dim shapes ahead and beside us!

Standing sure on the bridge, feet apart, hands on the wheel, you're staring straight ahead. Your manner calm, but your head awash with definitions: Meridian, Rhumb Line, the Great Circle, the Equivalency of Time. And you're in command, you're at the controls. Guiding this cumbersome vessel, huge as an office building, unwieldy as a blimp.

It rains. There's wind. Soon a swelling sea. We ride the trough between the swells and each time we surface the engine shudders. It's good to nestle beneath the command of one so sure of his direction; I'm proud to be standing beside you as your witness.

One by one the crew gets sick, fleeing below decks to lie down groaning, useless. But not us. Unaffected by the sea's rough course, we remain on the bridge, true sailors, riding out the storm.

Hours and hours you stand there steering. Glancing at the compass, peering through the rain-splattered window. You're pulling the ship along the imaginary path you worked out earlier, when the sun and moon showed which angles to use. You said there were times as a sailor when you served in four-hour shifts: four hours at the wheel, four hours in your cabin asleep. But there are no shifts now. Only hours and hours. Your hands gripping the wooden wheel. Your shoulder muscles knotting from the strain.

Each ship, you said, was like a live thing beneath your hands, a power so large, so prone to outside forces, that you could only revere it.

We ride the sea like confident breaststrokers, plunging into the waves, resurfacing for air. The long, long anchorage behind us. Our destination, to me, unclear. But the ship, she leaps! And I wouldn't leave you for worlds.

From "Navigation," *Word of Mouth*, 1996

SICK PIGEON
1991

SICK PIGEON

So I found this pigeon, eh? Lying beside the sandbox in the park. Whimpering. Trying to flap its wings. Looked like it'd been hit with a rock or maybe a dog got it. And all kinds of people around too. Everyone walking around it like it was a turd or something. Didn't want nothing to do with it. I couldn't figure it out. I mean there shoulda been a crowd around that bird all deciding what to do. I mean there's this poor sick pigeon in front of them probably going to die and nobody's doing a thing. What's happening is a big fat zero. What's happening is worse than nothing. I mean what's happening is a crime. The way nobody cares. Just like them mice in cages and them poor, helpless bunnies. Doing experiments on them like some weird horror movie. The way nobody cares about them either. Killing for no good reason.

So yeah, yeah Sybilla, it's a rotten world. Full to overflowing with crazies. So what's new?

But Jesus, I'm thinking, leaving a bird like that to die. In broad daylight. I mean people. They make me sick.

I started to cry when Christian first showed me it. Then he starts to cry so now there's two of us crouched over that bird bawling our eyes out. Mommy, is it going to die? He says and I says, no way ho-zay, not if I can help it. That kid has a heart like mine, can't stand to see a thing suffer.

So we brought it home, eh? Then all those jerks in the park started staring at us. Where before we coulda been dirt. I'm wrapping the pigeon in the baby's blanket and I'm putting it on the baby's lap in the stroller and everyone's giving us these disgusted looks like we was packing home a live rat or something. Moving away from us like we had the plague. Looking down on us. As usual. That's nothing new. Everyone's always looking down on us. Excepting maybe that worker Tony from when I was thirteen at the treatment centre. He never thumbed his nose at me, but then after a while he went away, never did hear from him again.

So what Sybilla? Tell us another one. You got some idea that shit and heartache ain't the price of admission?

Enough already, I says to myself, and pushes that bird out of the park, dragging Christian behind me. So there I am, eh? Slaving away with this buggy and not one of its wheels working right. And trying to shush the baby. She's got some bright idea that limp pigeon on her lap is a toy for playing with and all the way home she's banging at it with her bottle of Kool-Aid and screaming at me when I tell her to stop. End result is red Kool-Aid all over everything, ass to tea kettle, the baby, the pigeon, the blanket.

Then the sun comes out so suddenly it's a heat wave and we're three blocks from home and me, I'm sweating buckets and cursing myself, why'd I have to go leather today? Why couldn't I worn shorts and thongs like all them other mothers in the park, those ritzy bitches who wouldn't even give me the time of day even if I went begging for it.

You're up the creek without a paddle, Sybilla. Like always. You ain't running on a full tank.

So now I'm thinking, I hope this pigeon is grateful, what we're going through to save its life. It can thank its stars the day Sybilla found it and brought it home. And made it live. I make everything I find live. One way or another. Usually.

Live, you sucker. That's what I tell them, all the poor sick things. Take Gimp, for instance. Found her by the side of the road. Left for dead.

Ain't they all, you idiot. Ain't they all left for dead sometime? What about your own mother? Left for dead in a motel room. Drunk again. Choking on her own vomit.

Be quiet, I says to myself. I'll get to that. Right now it's animals I'm talking of. I'm talking of Gimp and how she'd been run over, her back all mangled. Can you picture what it's like to be run over?

S'cuse me while I throw up.

Yet there's cats all over the world regularly dragging themselves out from under cars, panting and gasping for air, looking for some kind person to save them. Lucky for Gimp she got me and not some creep who'd kick her in a ditch, not caring one small bit about her, probably getting a thrill out of watching her die. Lucky old Gimp. Took nearly all my welfare cheque for the vet bills and we had to eat canned soup for a week but I pulled her through. So now she can drag herself around pretty good. Even had three litters which explains all the cats I got around my place right now. Seventeen of them. Not including Gimp. Plus a couple of strays. I got a way with animals. They gravitate to me like shit to a blanket. They know I'll look after them, one way or another. They all know Sybilla's here when they need her.

But anywho, back to the pigeon. Time we get home this pigeon's not looking too good, got red Kool-Aid all over his body and breathing funny. I was getting real worried. I don't like to lose them. So we gave it a bath, eh? Figuring that might help. And Christian who's a gentle kid for being only three years old held it in a towel and patted it dry. The baby I threw in the tub.

We was just getting ready to find a bed for the bird, somewheres the cats couldn't get at it, and maybe try to give it some water, when I looks out the kitchen window and catch sight of Miss Hope, the Public Health Nurse, hustling her buns up the front path. Come for a visit, eh? Oh shit, I'm thinking, here comes trouble. So I says to Christian, quick Christian, take this bird and hide it somewheres in the bedroom away from the cats, we don't want Miss Hope finding it and causing a stink. She sees a sick pigeon in the house she won't shut up until Christmas. Next thing Miss Hope's rat-a-tatting on the kitchen door.

Are you crazy, Sybilla? Have you lost your marbles? There's garbage everywheres. Miss Hope takes one look in here she'll be yapping about disease and germs like always.

Jesus, I'm thinking, looking around the kitchen, what a holy mess. But that's the piss-off. These Miss Hopes and their like and every social worker I ever had the bad luck to know, they all figure when you're on welfare they can drop in on you any old time. They're like those surprise bombers in the TV war movies. Come out of nowhere. Can't wait to drop their bombs on you.

Bang, bang, you're dead, Sybilla.

No letting a person know. And they really got it in for single mothers. At least I coulda gotten rid of the cat dishes, maybe cleaned off the counter, made the place look decent. But not such luck. It's like they want to catch you with your pants down, always checking up on you to see if you're beating your kids yet. That's the one thing they live for, grabbing your kids. Like what happened to me. Grabbed from my mother when I was only eight years old. Just because she drank. They got no respect, all these do-good workers. I get about as much respect from them as a flea would get. Maybe less. How about that? Maybe they figure Sybilla's not even as good as a goddamned flea.

Stop it. You're breaking my heart.

So rat-a-tat goes this Miss Hope on the door, eh? And I'm stalling and calling, just a minute lady, and grabbing the baby outa the tub and making sure Christian's hid the bird good enough and find he's stashed it under the pillows on the bedroom floor.

Then again this Miss Hope's rapping on my door, only this time it's louder and she's hollering, Sybilla open the door please, I know you're in there.

Of course I'm in here, you dumb broad, I'm thinking, you figure this is a bank robbery, you're the cops got the place surrounded? You figure I'm holed up inside? Like when I was at the treatment centre, they way I used to barricade myself in the girl's dorm. All those workers making me do stuff like I was a slave or something. Wash the floors. Clean the toilets.

So I just get enough time to grab the bird and shove it under the kitchen sink and while I'm racing with it I'm noticing it's stopped breathing and I'm thinking, oh shit, I think it's dead. And this is really upsetting me, this is really twisting my socks. I mean I hardly get a chance to work on it and already it's croaking?

And this damned banging on the door, it ain't quitting. So then I finally open the door, got the baby hanging off my hip, still wearing my leathers, never did get time to change. And what does this Miss Hope lay on me but, I've come about your animals, Sybilla, we've been getting complaints again.

So there's this Miss Hope standing on my front porch, eh? Wearing this pink pantsuit, looking very shit hot, got about a ton of makeup on her wrinkles and red blush on her face about as red as a Valentine card. And moaning at me about having complaints again. And I'm going, Jesus, which one of these assholes around her finked on me this time?

I told them down at welfare last year when they first got me this dump, I told them then: I shouldn't be living in this prissy neighbourhood, you should have gotten me a joint in that new housing project where all the poor people live. Not shoving me in with all these high-class snots, always breathing down my neck, telling me how to live. I should be where all the real people are, in the housing project. They understand about saving sick animals and all the real problems of life.

But oh no, the social worker strung me some line about how this shitbox was all that was available and I was lucky I didn't have to live in some sleaze-bag motel. Yeah, great, I go, the only shitbox for miles around, stuck in the middle of a class act subdivision and I got to get it. A left-over shitbox at that. What they call an eyesore. Walls like paper, the roof leaking and none of the locks on the doors work right. Last winter it was so cold in here black mould started growing on the walls.

Poor old Sybilla. They figure that's all you're good for.

So I says to this Miss Hope, like who for instance ratted on me this time? I know for a fact who did it last time, that bitch down the road got shit for brains. Can't even control her own kids, always giving me the finger every time I go by. Talk about emotionally disturbed. And they said I was emotionally disturbed! Eight years old and thrown in a treatment centre for five years. Who wouldn't be disturbed?

Anywho, this Miss Hope says she can't tell me who complained, it's confidential information. *Confidential information!* She says she's just come to tell me the SPCA inspectors are coming around any minute now to make an investigation, there's been complaints, they say, of a large number of dead or dying cats lying in my front yard. She says. She says. Gimme a break.

So I slam the door in her face, eh? Get out of here you douche-bag, I'm screaming, my cats are all in beautiful shape, you got the wrong house, the only thing not in great shape in here is me and that's because bitches like you won't get off my back.

That fixed her. She took off then, got in her car slamming the door and drove off.

You tell her Sybilla. What does she know? Thinks she's so great in her pink pantsuit. You tell her where to get off. You tell them all where to get off.

I will, I'm thinking, pissed right out of my tree. I mean, no one's telling me how to live.

So what happens next, eh? But the baby starts howling and pretty soon there's Christian hanging off my leg and starting to cry. And that's all I'm needing. I start bawling too. Me and Christian and the baby, we're sitting on the kitchen floor, leaning against the cupboards and we're bawling our eyes out. It just ain't fair. Why can't they leave us alone? Just because I'm a single mother. Just because I'm only nineteen. Just because the kids got different fathers, I don't even want to think about those jerks. Just because I've got a kind heart.

Poor Sybilla. Got an "m" on your forehead the size of a billboard light. Poor, poor girl.

And then the cats start coming round us, there on the floor, frantic like, some of them purring, some of them hissing at each other. I know they're hungry, they finished the last bag of crunchies a couple of days back and my cheque's not due till Thursday. But I never have enough money, it all goes on these animals. Someone's got to look after them. All the SPCA does is kill them, right? Someone's got to care.

So then I'm remembering about that pigeon, eh? And I'm feeling bad thinking it's dead. I take it out from under the sink and have a look at it. Got to keep pushing the cats away, they're thinking it's something to eat. But the bird is so pretty, kind of a silvery grey colour with blue flecks in it. The sun's shining on it through the window and it's almost sparkling, like it was covered with tiny blue lights. So I start patting and stroking its back. This makes Christian and the baby get real quiet and stop their bawling. So there we are on the kitchen floor, all looking at the bird on my lap. The cats cruising around, still trying to get at the poor harmless thing. And I'm thinking, we'll have to bury it, have a little ceremony. Christian likes having a ceremony. He always puts one of his toys in the grave, a Hot Wheels car or something he's made out of Lego. So then I start thinking how everything's so sad. I mean, there's my poor dead Mom, never did get to see her again after they took me away. There's those guys who knocked me up then buggered off. You know, I'm thinking of all the miserable junk that passes for some kind of life when all of a sudden the pigeon gives a shudder and starts flapping its wings, trying to stand up. And now I'm so happy, I'm going, it's a miracle. This pigeon is alive after all, he's going to live. And I say to Christian, Christian we got to get him some water, it looks like this pigeon is going to make it. Maybe it had passed out or something before, maybe it was only sleeping.

So then I get the pigeon a drink, eh? I fill up the baby's bottle with water figuring to put the nipple into the bird's mouth the way I do with the sick cats, give them water that way. And I'm feeling so great, eh? That I only get mildly twisted when I see the cop car pull up in front of the house, got its lights flashing red and blue. Then the SPCA van. Then Miss Hopeless in her dinky blue car. All of them crowding in front of my house.

And I'm thinking, it looks like I'll just be getting enough time to push the kitchen table against the door before they all come storming up the path. So I go to Christian, quick Christian, help me shove this table against the door, we don't want anyone bursting in on us and bothering us when we got important work to do. There's a sick pigeon here needing water and what do all these assholes know about that!

ROB'S GUNS & AMMO

There's this old guy, maybe forty, forty-five got this business in town? I figure he's my Dad. I mean, he looks like me. Small. Skinny. Got the same pointy nose. Only difference is his hair is brown and mine's blonde. Well, yellow really. But the roots, they'd be about the same.

It'd be real easy to prove we was related. Just stand us side by side. Just stand us together in front of a mirror. I mean, any idiot would have to say, "Yeah, Sybilla, he's gotta be your Dad. No doubt about it." I mean, shit, we could be twins if he wasn't such an old fart.

And the name's right, too. Rob. Says so right on his sign. ROB'S GUNS & AMMO. Is that proof or what?

Well, all right, maybe I don't know for sure he's my Dad. I mean, my Mom, all she ever told me before she died was his name. But I've been putting two and two together. His name and how he looks—plus where I was born, only twenty miles from here—and coming up with one, big happy family. Which is about time. After all those years in Alderwood, that treatment centre I was in for screwed-up kids.

So don't laugh, asshole. Is it my fault my Mom was a drunk and I got taken away? Gimme a break.

Eight years old and thrown in a treatment centre. You'd be disturbed, too, after going through that. I mean, that place was like a prison. All we ever did there was clean the floors. Do the dishes. What they called "functioning." And talk about our feelings. Talk about our feelings *to death*.

Don't ever ask me how I'm feeling. Don't ever say those words to me. I'm likely to go strange on you. I must of sat at the kitchen table at Alderwood a thousand times having to *talk about my feelings*. Having to explain why I figured some worker was a douche-bag. Why some other kid deserved to have her Barbie swiped. Over and over. It never stopped, that talking. Every time I'd turn around some worker would be on my case. *How do you feel about* this, Sybilla? *How do you feel about* that, Sybilla? It got so's the sound of those words made me wanna puke. And when I was thirteen and a half and ran away for the last time? What did my social worker lay on me but, *How do you feel about going to a group home, Sybilla?*

Feelings. It's like some disease all these workers got. Even Miss Hope, the public health nurse always banging on my door? Checking up on germs and corruption? She's a feeling freak, too. "How does it *feel*, Sybilla, to be on welfare?

"Oh terrific," I go, thinking you dumb broad, how do you think it *feels*? It feels like shit. Shitty. The pits.

But is she satisfied with that? No way. She's got to go for the throat. "No really, Sybilla, how does it *really* make you *feel*?"

Lights all flashing like this was some TV quiz show and I get the big prize if I answer right. Like stars on the fridge at Alderwood. Tokens. Ten tokens gets you a chocolate bar. But first you gotta say the right words about your feelings. First you gotta slobber after their praise.

A hundred tokens gets you taken to a movie by the favourite worker. That's a laugh! I mean, who'd ever have a favourite worker? That's like having a favourite spider. Or poisonous snake.

So I'm up to here with all these yo-yos. With all their talk. They're paid to do that. Ask about your *feelings*. Pretend they care. I figure it's time I had my own family. I mean, besides Christian and the baby. I figure it's time I got my Dad to take care of me the way he shoulda done all those years ago.

Only thing is, I got to convince this guy Rob he's my Dad.

So every time we stand out front ROB'S GUNS & AMMO I says to Christian, look Christian, see that man in there? He's probably your Grandpa.

And Christian, who's three, he gets all excited jumps up and down starts waving his arms the way he did last Christmas at Santa Claus in the parade.

Which isn't far off. Santa Claus, I mean. I figure Rob's gotta be rich. Having a store like that. He's gotta be loaded. The stuff in the two big windows for starters. Megabucks. Stuff for hunting and fishing. Basketball hoops. Expensive running shoes like what the sports stars wear on TV. Hats. All kinds of junk for camping. Stoves. Sleeping bags hanging from the ceiling.

With all the money Rob's got he could start me a kennel so's I don't have all my animals in the house no more. Causing Miss Hopeless to get all twisted about the smell every time she barges in for a visit. You'd think she was my best friend or something. All the time she spends with us. Getting me to clean up the place just like you-know-where.

"I'm too busy," I go. "I got all these animals to look after."

But she's always at me. Yak. Yak. Yak. About the baby's Pampers, are they changed enough? About keeping stuff off the floor so's Christian and the baby don't put dirt in their mouths and get diarrhea.

"Get me a kennel," I go, "then there won't be dirt on the floor. Or get welfare to get me a decent house. Get all these jerks we got for neighbours off my back, then we can talk about dirt on the floor."

So I figure having Rob for a Dad would end all the hassle. It's the perfect solution. That's why we hang around his store so much. Nearly every day. Getting the nerve to go in and introduce ourselves.

Only problem is, how do I do it? I mean, we're total strangers to him, right? Do I march in the store and say, "Hi there, remember way back when? ... A girl called Rita? ... That was my mother ... well, you knocked her up ... "

Sure I'm gonna say that. Get real. That sounds like I'm some nut case out on a day pass. Like I'm brain-damaged.

Or how 'bout: "Hey Rob, ever wonder if you had a kid someplace you didn't know about?"

Ha! What kind of guy is gonna own up to that?

So that's why I've been chickenshit about going in, eh? I mean, how do I start a conversation? How do I prove to him he's my Dad? How do I tell him about us so he won't say *fuck off asshole*? He could just say I'm crazy, get outa here, get lost, who'd want you for a daughter?

This Rob, he could say anything he likes. I mean, it's really important to me he's my Dad and I don't want to scare him off.

I'd even settle for some money from him. Enough to get off welfare and start me a kennel. And maybe a visit with him now and then. That'd be okay. You know, like at Christmas? Or my birthday?

So this Rob, he's my number one project now. Lots of times I seen him in the store. Hanging stuff on the racks. Dusting all the guns he's got in a glass case behind the counter. Helping customers. One time I saw him walking down Beacon Avenue around lunch time. Me and Christian and the baby in the stroller, we wheeled around and followed him like he was a magnet. Right into the Beacon Café. Even stood behind him in the take-out line. With my high-heeled boots on we was about the same size. He got himself a bowl of chili, two buns, a salad, and a coffee. Christian and me, we split a Coke. Sat in the booth across from him but didn't have the nerve to say hello.

A couple of times he's smiled at me through the window but not like he knew me or anything. The same kind of smile he gives the guys who buy guns and fishing rods.

And I can't stop thinking about him. Rob. Like where does he live and how it'll be when he knows I'm his daughter. And all the stuff he'll give us outa the store. And all of us going to the Beacon Café for lunch. And how he's buying.

So we was going along like this for a couple of weeks. Hanging out front of the store and smiling at Rob when we could see him. You know, trying to get him used to us and hoping pretty soon he'd want to meet us.

And then last Monday something really weird happened. Something that's like made the whole story a whole lot more interesting. For me anyways.

We was standing out front the store like usual. Killing time. Waiting to go down the welfare office. Our cheque was supposed to be in at ten.

The baby, she was asleep in her stroller and Christian, he had his Hot Wheels car, going vroom vroom back and forth on the window ledge. Rob, I could see him, he was inside behind the counter working at some papers.

I was just gonna say to Christian, come on Christian, I guess we stood here long enough for one day, when out the store in a big hurry comes this fat old broad. Purple sweatsuit, frizzy grey hair. Comes right up to me.

She's got this mean look on her face and she says, "Can I help you?" Acting like she owns the place.

You got to see her. One of these sour jobs. All squished-up face like a social worker I had once. Doesn't take me two seconds to hate her.

So I says to her, "No thanks, we're just standing here deciding which parked car we're gonna steal." I thought it was funny.

But she didn't. She's sucking lemons. "Well," she says, "you been hanging out front the store quite a lot lately and if you don't have business here then you'd better leave."

"It's a free country," I go, or some such garbage. "I can stand here if I want to."

Then she goes off on this big speech, eh? About how the front of the store is *her* property and how I'm trespassing and if I want to hang out somewheres why don't I go to the park down the wharf?

And I'm looking the other way, not at her, like I used to do at Alderwood, to all the workers. Pretending I'm deaf. Acting like it's all one big gi-normous yawn till finally I gets sick of her yapping and tells her to fuck off which I probably shouldn't a done 'cause then she gets all twisted and red in the face and starts screaming at us right there on the street. Screaming about my *language* and what kind of mother would talk like that and how we're all alike—whatever that means—and on and on till finally I says, "Well, I got a right to be here. I know Rob," figuring that would shut her up. What an idiot thing to say. Does Sybilla ever keep her trap shut? Like shoot my brains out and I still wouldn't know I was dead.

So this old bag goes, "What Rob?"

"Rob inside," I go, trying to sound as mean as she looks. "Rob who owns the store."

"I own the store," she says, "and there is no Rob. That's just the name of the store when I bought it."

"Yeah sure," I go, "well who's that?" And I'm pointing past her through the window.

So this old broad turns around and has herself a look, eh? Then she laughs, a snarly kind of laugh. "That's Earl," she says. "Earl who works for me. What you want with Earl?"

"Don't give me that shit," I says 'cause I don't believe her one bit and then Christian starts bawling and grabbing my leg. "Now look what you've done," I'm shouting. "You've scared my kid. I could get the cops after you for child abuse, you know, frightening little kids."

And I picks up Christian to make it look good and by now people are slowing down and stopping on the sidewalk, having a look at us.

The old bag turns around then shaking her head and storms back in the store. Slams the door so hard the little bell comes crashing onto the sidewalk. And the people who was watching us? After a few minutes, they just kind of melt away.

Then I'm just like Christian, I can't stop bawling. Standing there on the sidewalk out front of Rob's store I'm bawling like an idiot. Everything's got so mixed up. Everything's got so crazy.

So the only thing I can figure to do, eh? Is stay standing there till I'm good and ready to leave. No old bag is gonna scare me off, I'm thinking. No douche-bag pushes Sybilla around and gets away with it.

So we stand there for maybe another fifteen minutes just to make our point. Don't even turn around and look in the store window though I can tell the old bag is gunning me, watching every move I make.

And when we finally start heading down Beacon Avenue it's because I want to. Not because we've been told to leave. It's because it's ten by now and our cheque's in down at the welfare office.

So that's what we do next, eh? Get my cheque then head over to the pet store to get it cashed. So what if I blew it all on fish? Well, nearly all of it. That's my business.

Tropical fish. And all the junk that goes with them. The tank. Food. Little castles that go in the tank. And special white rocks that come in a plastic bag. I got six of them. We got so much stuff we had to take a taxi home.

So it's four days later and we're still hanging out front ROB'S GUNS & AMMO. I figure that old bag was lying to me. About Rob being Earl. About it being *her* store. About everything. She's got it in for me, that I know for sure. And I still figure Rob's my Dad. It won't be long before he figures it out, too. Then everything'll be okay. Don't ask me how I know this, I just do.

So far the old bag has hassled us no more but I seen her peeking at us a couple of times. From behind a rack of ski jackets. And Rob, I still see him every day. Not paying much attention to us. Working away in his store.

A couple of times a cop car has gone by real slow, having a good look at us standing out front. Hasn't done nothing yet. And Miss Hopeless the other day? She asks me how come I was hanging around Rob's so much. But do I talk to workers? Do I spill my guts for free? You already know the answer to that one.

So it's giving me a big laugh. I mean all these people hovering around—the cops, Miss Hopeless, the old bag—they're just like the fish in my new tank. Doing all this quiet cruising. Day after day. Just waiting to see what old Sybilla's gonna do next. Holding their breaths, all nervous, in case I go strange on them.

But maybe you think I'm cracked, eh? All this stuff about Rob being my Dad? Well, all I got to say about that is: blow it out your ear. I'm like one of my dogs with a bone when I know a thing for sure. I won't ever let go of it no matter what. No one's gonna change my mind about Rob. Not in a million years. Not ever. So don't even try.

The Loneliest Sound You'll Ever Hear

Jimmy Silvey rides the range. This time he's in a bar drinking alone, the tall, rumpled-looking man in the corner by the pool table watching the three Indian women. They wear different combinations of black and purple like a bruise and give Jimmy Silvey quick, sharp looks that are not meant to be noticed. He nurses his beer, pretending to ignore them, and listens to their conversation. Mostly they are saying what a bastard some guy called Lewis is and then they begin a game of pool. They take a long time choosing their pool cues, all the while pulling at their sweaters like some kind of signal and blowing cigarette smoke out of their nostrils like mad horses. Jimmy takes the one in the middle, the fat one, not usually chosen, Carol-Ann. And leaves her somewhere in northern Alberta before the child comes.

Another time. Coming home to his mother's dump after two years of wandering. Wheeling his ruined blue pick-up off the ferry and out into the cool grey drizzle, his aged dog wheezing on the seat beside him, her old tail wagging as soon as they hit the coast and Jimmy Silvey, bringing his dog home to die and himself home to rest a while.

He can see himself in his lone truck, rainwater flying up from the wheels as he crests the quiet town below, the lone stranger riding through the deserted October streets, a silent man out of nowhere and with nothing but the contents of his saddle bag, a sensitive man with a dying dog and an old mother, his collar turned up and his baseball cap pulled low against the big thoughts eating up his brain and the small adventures squeezing out his soul, riding into town on this desolate Sunday morning, the only sounds, the rain splatting his tires, his wheezing dog, the suck of his cigarette.

To plead his case. Only that his soul is a boiling black cloud that won't be stayed, a train that's moving on. Away but never to a thing. The smooth, vacant road, he says, it calls, he's got to wander. The loneliest sound you'll ever hear is the wind high up in the cold firs that line Jimmy Silvey's road, is the thin, distant cry from Carol-Ann in the bare motel room, her heart slowly tearing.

Ultimately the heart. The heart of Jimmy Silvey, his reason why. He cannot answer the question precisely, never having had any luck in this world. Cheerless drifter. Blown like dust before the wind, whirlpools of ugly emotions, blown by his own restless soul across arid landscapes, through empty, haunting forests. To land in dry unexpected places. Moving on.

At times to his mother. Having lost all sense of him, year after year, never knowing when he'll turn up. Jimmy Silvey parks his truck on the wet grass in front of his mother's house and quiets the dog who has struggled to sit up, a look of expectation on her face. A large heavy dog, her face covered with white hairs, her tail thumping on the ripped vinyl seat.

The same old house. Grey stucco walls, wet concrete steps, the wooden front door. The soggy poverty of the place. And the garden, too, drowned: a ragged chrysanthemum, a small drooping bush. Jimmy Silvey imagines the lonely woman inside, her life sodden with boredom, imagines his mere ruined presence bringing joy, like an unexpected gift.

This time she's at the kitchen counter buttering toast. Jimmy Silvey comes up behind her, quiet as a cat, and calls her name so softly she thinks it is her own sad desire speaking to her. But there he surely is, her own poor Jimmy, never having had any luck in this world. He's thinner than she remembers, his clothes dirty, the smell of him strong like gasoline, sour like sweat, and thinning on the top she notices and sagging beneath the eyes as if his whole face was hollowing in. Home at last and doesn't he look as if he needs someone to love him?

Then the dog. Jimmy Silvey helps her out of the truck. His mother, wrapped now in a cardigan against the forlorn morning, is with him too, offering the dog pieces of buttered toast. "Who's a good dog now?" she's saying, stroking the bony back, kissing the dog on the head. "Who's a good old thing?"

We're all she has, Jimmy thinks, and feels the weight of that responsibility descend upon him like an angry black cloud, feels the storm it causes in his heart whenever he cannot give what is needed.

He stays the winter. To rest a while. With his dog and his mother, the only beings in Jimmy Silvey's world who love him without question, without reason.

And then it's spring. Jimmy Silvey spends the last two weeks of April working on the truck's transmission out in his mother's driveway. The world suddenly a brighter place, everything alive around him: flowers, birds, dogs, kids on bikes, pensioners pulling at weeds in their derelict gardens, all of them shaking off the soggy winter, putting hopeful faces towards the sun and taking deep breaths of the sudden sweet air and smiling.

And Jimmy Silvey's heart fills with the same impulse of hope and his thoughts turn towards Alberta and Carol-Ann and the baby. He plays the truck radio as he works and his soul, it seems to swell as he listens to the music, some rock and roll tune about love and good times. And he gets an idea. A golden idea that's pulling him away from the dreary time with his mother, now that he's rested. Some bright dream scene about things being all right with Carol-Ann. He can almost see himself happy, riding into that northern Alberta town to see her, arriving like a surprise out of nowhere and the brightness he might possibly bring. Having dreamed up the next place to go.

And so on the first Monday in May he loads into the truck his wheezing dog who did not die and kisses his sad mother good-bye and heads out towards the ferry, impatient to be on his way and thinking of Carol-Ann and the child, she must be two by now, and wondering if they are still in the same motel or if they have moved or if he can find them.

Time passes. Jimmy Silvey wanders the range, a drifter along Route 401. His truck, broken down, is left for dead by the side of the road, his dog buried in a ditch along the way. Carol-Ann is from another time.

A man of few words, he hitches rides, does odd jobs, sleeping roadside when it's warm, on floors during winter. Surprising no one. Jimmy's eyes are rigid pools finding a point and moving towards it. His heart is an empty husk blown on its stubborn way.

Alone in the mountains for two weeks, Jimmy Silvey hears a train whistle. The loneliest sound you'll ever hear, he thinks. It sounds like a thin, distant cry. He walks towards it furtively, fists clenched at his side. Deliberately through rough salal, slippery ravines, over rotting logs. It's a bright sunlit morning yet he seems to move under the cover of night, in fear, watching the vacant forest for signs of his personal doom: murderers with guns, knives, ravaging animals, the sudden upheaval of old timber.

He wears his hair slicked back beneath a baseball cap, a cheap brown suit, tied at the waist with a rope. Carries a slender pack over his shoulders, covers his eyes with cheap wraparound sunglasses, disguising himself against the treachery without, the emptiness within. Jimmy Silvey is hurrying through every obstacle towards that crying sound, a man, for the moment, with somewhere to go.

All the Good and Beautiful Forces

Hey, let me tell you, the trips have been heavy. But like I say to the young ones, the ones with spikes for hair and pins through their noses, enlightenment is a calling, not for everyone. And if they can settle down long enough to hear the truth I tell them this: some people got to be plumbers or brain surgeons and some people got to sell insurance or be gynecologists even, peering up women's snatches all day. But if your own true calling, like mine, is the road to Nirvana, is that drive for Oneness, then you've got to hang in there through the good and the bad. You've got to push through every level of understanding you can and pocket for yourself every bit of universal wisdom like I done. Then you'll be able to dance.

It's probably one of the hardest roads to travel, I tell them, and the way ain't easy, but if you work at it, you can probably get there.

Like for me, the first time nearly blew me away. Seems like a million years ago now. There I was eighteen and still with fuzz on my face and well on my way to oblivion when these two guys from SFU turned me onto some Colombian Gold. Under a bridge on the Fraser River. I was so dumb I thought they were taking me on a canoe trip. Shit, my mother even packed me a lunch. We'd stopped to rest and get out of the rain and just as I was opening up the wax paper around my sandwich, this guy Jim pulls out the Zig-Zags and a bag of grass. I hardly knew what the stuff was. Heroin, I thought, alarm bells going. Even expected the cops to swoop down, you know, the usual paranoid stuff. But that wasn't what did me in. It was later on, after I'd gotten used to inhaling and holding my breath, when the three of us were standing on the muddy bank grooving on the drizzle and the way the water flowed in time to "Jumpin' Jack Flash" on Jim's transistor radio and this other guy, Brian, I think his name was, said, "Life is terminal, man."

I mean those words hit me like a rocket. I nearly passed out from the truth. I said it out loud, "You live, you die. That's it. There ain't nothing else." I mean I couldn't get over it. My mouth must have hung down to my knees. Brian just nodded his head like he'd let me in on the big joke and I was his latest fool. I guess his trip was ripping the cobwebs from the eyes of snot-nosed innocents like me, but it had an effect, I felt it right down to my core, and all the while I'm trying to get a handle on this heavy revelation my mind's so stretched I was seeing stars throbbing on the leaves of trees, souls fluttering in the breasts of sea gulls.

I was so twisted I tried to put my lunch bag over my head, blot it all out, wipe away the awful truth: "You live, you die." I spent weeks after that, going from class to class at the university almost scared to think, but this one idea wouldn't go away and I knew it *never* would. Life was just one big cartoon with Woody Woodpecker at the end of it shrieking like a maniac, "Bid-di-dit, bid-di-dit, bid-di-dit. That's all folks."

For years that woodpecker kept howling at me and that red head kept turning up, man did it ever! I'd never know what form it would take and then, later on, it settled on my old lady Red but by then it was screaming a different tune: "Do *this* Wilson. Do *that* Wilson," she'd order all the time like some kind of torment.

But, hey, like I said, the path to enlightenment takes work. You don't give up because of irritating shit like woodpeckers or being afraid about living and dying. You got to be on top of all that. Grease the old sy-nap-sees. Get in the groove. That's what I did.

Sure there were bad trips. Ever read Camus on acid?

It was Osley's Blue at somebody's beachhouse. The world went all melted plastic but this chick I was with had Camus in her pack, *The*

Myth of Sisyphus. "Here," she said, "feed on this." After a while I managed to understand what I was reading but that eating idea took hold and pretty soon words started crawling off the page and coming up my arms like worms, like broken spider's legs. And then this one word, "meaninglessness," poked itself right into my eyeballs and into my ears and up my nose so that before long it had gotten into my head, like rot, and taken over. And then everything meant nothing, a big fat zero. So I figured, well if that's the case, there's no way I'm going to push a rock up a hill for the rest of my life, not like my old man, the bathtub salesman. Hell.

So you see, plenty of good things can come out of a bad trip. It was about that time I dropped out of second year. Hey, if everything was meaningless, I might as well get a lid of dope, ride the Cosmic Elevator, right? Cast my thoughts into the vast useless ether, enjoy the ride. It was the best thing I ever did. I moved in with a bunch of freaks, made candles, sold dope, got by that way.

Yeah, I sure took to dope, must have had the right disposition for it. I mean it was my number one teacher. I learned stuff on dope it would take a dude maybe a thousand years to figure out straight.

Love is part of it too so I've always been into that. Back then, I tell you, it was the Golden Age. Peace. Love. Dove. Every chick would put out right away, no questions asked, just because you were beautiful. I was calm all the time.

Now and then my old man used to track me down, rattle his tonsils about my hair, about my dropping out of school. My Jesus robe really bugged his ass. I used to say, "Hey man, if you really love me it doesn't matter what I look like." "Bullshit," he'd say, "what's love got to do with it? You weren't born to turn into a godammed vegetable. What are you going to do with the rest of your life?" "Hey, what's the sweat?" I'd say. "When you're dead who gives a fuck?" "Think of your mother," he'd say, by now sounding like a wood-pecker, "you're breaking her heart." I'd try to explain. "Hey man, we're just travelling different roads, that's all. You got a bathtub on your

39

back. Me, I'm carrying the wisdom of the universe and anyway what have hearts got to do with it? Trouble with you," I'd tell him, "you don't know what living is. All you care about is selling bathtubs and cutting the lawn and drinking martinis." "That's not true," he'd say, "you just wait until you have children of your own. You just wait till they break your heart." "Shit, man," I'd answer, "nobody owns their kids. What do you think I am, a godammed goldfish?"

One time he actually smoked some dope with us. In this dump we had on Fourth Avenue. Him in his tie and shirt, his fat belly hanging over his pants, that bathtub on his back, sitting crosslegged around the sand candles with us in the dark. Said he wanted to find out what all this "marijuana business" was about. "Far out!" I said. But stoned, he looked hassled. I could see right into his soul like it was a plate glass window at a department store. Just bathtubs and toaster ovens in there; he was a real disappointment.

And then it turned heavy. It must have been the paregoric we soaked the joints in. Before long everything in the room was on a tilt, like I was standing at the bottom of a mountain and my old man and everybody else was on top. I felt like I was being crushed, right in my chest, and I couldn't breathe. And then the mountain turned into a giant bathtub, the whole room was a white enamel bathtub and it started to fill up with water and my father was grinning, he had teeth like chrome bathroom fixtures and I kept yelling, "Pull the plug, we're gonna drown." But.everyone else seemed to be swimming just fine, all of them like monster goldfish, even my fat old man, he could swim the best. But me, I was drowning. I was gonna die in my father's bathtub and the only thing that could save me was to get out of there and never go near a bathtub or my old man again. And that's what I did.

Anytime I'd happen to see my old man after that I'd get that drowning feeling all over again and have to split, and have to swim for my life.

Fuck, shit, piss, eh? Some trip. Hey, but in living your life there are some things you've got to avoid if you want to stay calm. For a while bathtubs were easy to miss but I had a harder time with woodpeckers. Like for years I was falling in love about once a week. It was all right for the longest time but then one night this big, blonde chick from California, Loralee, showed up with her dog and a load of mescaline and it was from Loralee that my path led directly to Red.

Loralee was a turn-on, too bad she didn't stick around. She wore a poncho and cowboy boots and when we got it on her dog would howl like a wolf, the whole world knew what was happening. And Loralee was a real noisy chick, too. Screamed and shouted making love and then wanted more. Nearly did me in. But I could have stayed with her forever. She'd kind of look after me, cook me food, brush my hair. So I followed her to Hornby Island and met some guys she knew there who were into agriculture. There's where I stayed and learned to grow dope.

The country's the place to be, birds and all that natural shit. Stoned, Loralee read my Tarot cards, said I always drew the Death card and that meant I was one heavy dude. Hey, that's me, Wilson, the heavy dude! But I didn't like the idea of carrying Death around on my back. I should have known that the woodpecker was coming close. Just as soon as life and death come into the picture, shaking things up and demanding meaning. I should have known that before long I'd run into Red. It was my Karma.

It happened this one time when I'd been living for ages with the freaks on Hornby Island, minding my own business, growing dope, staying calm. There was this weird guy lived down the road a ways called Ken-Zen and he was into heavy machinery, power wagons, tractors, industrial chain saws. I don't know how it happened but Ken-Zen and I ended up having this contest to see who could chop the most firewood, him with his chain saw or me with an axe. So everybody came. It was a real event, all the freaks and their ladies in long flowered skirts and shawls. This Ken-Zen had said that going back to the land was a pile of shit and he was going to prove that machines were stronger than men. Can't think now why I was picked to take him on but I did and it was a real bummer. He was light years ahead of me with the wood and I nearly broke my goddamned arms trying to keep up with him. After he'd won he strutted off to his cabin laughing like an idiot and I was left in the pile of half-split wood feeling like a useless bastard if ever there was one.

But then there was this chick, someone's friend from the Mainland. I'd never seen her before. Her name, she said, was Red on account of her red hair and the red aura she always had around her. I should have flashed on the woodpecker but I was too freaked out over losing the contest to notice and then Red was being so nice to me. She was real calm, like a soft swollen lake, and she didn't say much that day as we roamed through the woods, except, "I love you, Wilson." She said it a couple of times. "I love you, Wilson." We made love in a clearing covered with moss and wildflowers, shooting stars and some tiny blue flowers were all about, and maybe it was the dope, but that day I guess I loved her too.

Before long she made herself my lady. She always wore this grey blanket made into a long skirt and a black and green lumber jacket. She drank Calona Red for breakfast. Next thing I knew, I'd knocked her up.

Red knew of this place called Sombrio Beach, just up the coast from Sooke, where there were some empty shacks on the beach. It was getting to be spring so we went there. We found a cabin that was pretty rotten in this cove but figured we could fix it up with driftwood and some plastic. Everyone else was doing that down there. We were getting welfare so the money was no sweat. It was a gas to hitch a ride into Sooke for supplies and get pots and pans from the Sally Ann and sacks of brown rice and pinto beans from the health food store and bring the stuff back to our shack on the beach. It was neat in there, like a fort I'd had as a kid. We made a bed out of cedar boughs and an old sleeping bag and I fixed up some shelves using flat pieces of driftwood I found on the beach.

It was incredible, too, having all that welfare bread. The dope you could buy! And we lived pretty good, got rock cod off the beach and mussels and clams off the rocks. Now and then straight campers would hike down the cliff to the beach for the day and then find they couldn't carry all their stuff back with them. It was like Christmas then, we'd be given hot dogs and buns, jugs of wine, Oreo cookies, bags of potato chips. One time we were left three sirloin steaks. Shit, did we have a feast that night! During the time on the beach we did a fair bit of acid and when it came summer and got hot we went naked all day. Boy, did that blow the campers' minds! Yeah, we were a real community of freaks down there, living calm and easy. But then it got heavy.

Winter came and the rain. That place was like living inside a plastic bag. Everything was wet all the time and then Red started bitching like a regular fishwife. I'd seen it coming all summer; she'd get her bird claws into me over every little thing. Like where was I going whenever I'd wander down the beach with Anabel, two shacks down, or why didn't I come straight home after a trip to Sooke, how come I had to stay away for a week? She started acting like she owned me. You'd think I wore a three-piece suit all day or something and then that shitless winter she started screaming, "Why don't you get a job, Wilson? Why don't we get a proper house, Wilson?" I sure found out what that red aura of hers meant. Trouble, man.

Here she was turning into that woodpecker, that "you live, you die" woodpecker and making all the stuff in between a colossal bad trip. And there I was in her cage somehow, in the goddamned bird cage with her, and I couldn't get out because I was tied. She had that kid in her stomach and it was mine. I was tied because I thought then I wanted that kid.

I did acid the night Red finally had it. I felt like I was on the moon. Just whirling around in space. There was this storm crashing branches outside the cabin and I thought it was meteor and stars we were banging into. It was so cold in there, too. The beach wood was so wet it only fizzled when I lit it.

The guy from the next cabin came in and did some chants with an eagle feather over Red. He was a skinny guy with red acne crud all over his face but he sure had soul, the way he said those chants, all about spirits and stars and the universe. It was heavy duty, made me think of God. And just one candle burning, too, made me think of nativity scenes on Christmas cards. It was about that time of the year, and for a moment I felt swollen up with warmth like I was Joseph and Red was Mary and maybe this kid inside her was another Jesus about to be born, my Jesus, my boy. I rode on that thought for most of the night until Red, with her usual woodpecker screech started complaining about her pains and shrieking so much I had to go outside and sit under a tree. That frosted me off. In all that rain. And then that drowning business started all over again. I was sitting in a bathtub and all the rain was going to fill it up and I was going to drown. The guy with the eagle feather came outside just as I was yelling, "Get out, get out, the ship's sinking," and he grabbed me and pulled me from the water. "It's a girl," he said. "Vishnu Meadowlark."

Not long after that I split. I don't know what I expected of that kid, maybe to come varooming out on a bike or something, but I sure wasn't into all that crying and stink. Red carried on with her wood-pecker ways, killing any good feeling I'd ever had about the kid, or her, even. She wanted me to do all the work, too, like hike up the cliff about fifteen times a day to get a ride to Sooke for supplies. And it was winter, too. "Get some food, Wilson." "Gather some wood, Wilson." "Here, Wilson, look after the baby." Shit, man, I ain't no-body's slave. And Red got so fat after the kid, she ballooned up like a giant spider, and all the time shouting orders at me, breaking my balls. I had to get out of there.

Lucky for me my grandmother croaked about then and left me some dough. I got the hell away from Red and that kid and did it ever feel good to split out of that cage, like I'd busted out of jail. No more of Red's screaming, no more hauling wood, freezing my ass in that shack. I headed for Vancouver.

Before I knew it Anabel from the beach had found me. That's chicks for you. Soon as they sniff any free bread they're on you like a dirty blanket. Anabel kept feeding me a line about how much she loved me and what a heavy dude I was. Hey, I wasn't immune! I let her be my lady for a while but deep down I figured, no way was a chick going to get the best of me again.

Anyways, after going to Europe on my grandmother's money and then living in Mexico for a while, and then in an Oregon commune, I finally ended up on Salt Spring Island, where I've been ever since. Living by myself, staying clear of people trying to change me.

But, hey, the trips I've had. Nothing too heavy, though, just small beautiful adventures, and no more of that woodpecker stuff either, none of that.

But I don't know where the time's gone, months just fly by like fenceposts on a highway, whole years are a distant, golden blur. It's like a speeded-up movie, but a good movie, one that's beautiful. And anyways, time's not where it's at. These days I'm into dancing, any kind of dancing. I'm into joy and celebration; I'm going to dance till I ain't no more. There's so much to feel good about, so many reasons to dance. I got these two cats, Sam and Annie, they're like people, follow me all round my place, We communicate, we understand each other. And my garden. I grow tomatoes, kohlrabi, potatoes and kale, all organic, none of that chemical crap in my food.

But people, when they see me now at the Saturday morning market, they think I'm just another old hippie selling candles. It slays me. They think I'm brain-damaged, living in some time warp from the sixties. Shit with sauce, they look at my bald head, at my beard, and they think I'm some kind of basket case.

But, hey, they don't know what these eyes are seeing, they can't ever understand what I know. I'll bet none of them can get up and dance whenever the spirit moves them. I'm open to forces they'll never even dream about.

Like last week in the drug store. I get this rush, a golden glow all through my nerve endings and I hadn't even smoked dope or done anything. Just straight and crazy. But warm, man, but hot to dance. So I grab this old broad who's stocking the shelves and try to twirl her down the aisle to the Muzak but shit if she doesn't scream, her old face just cracked like concrete. "Help! Help!" she yells. "Feel the spirit," I say, "get in the Cosmic Groove, lady, we're all children of the Universe," but she grabs this bottle of Pepto-Bismol and cracks it across my head. Pretty soon there's the pharmacist pulling at my poncho and next thing I know I'm in the back of a cop car. "Take it easy, Wilson," the cop says. "Settle down, Wilson."

But that's the trouble with people, they're always freaking out over small shit like that. They got souls the size of shrivelled peas. That old broad said I smelled. But it was her that stank, must have had about a gallon of perfume on her, strong enough to make you gag. Put a match to her and she'd explode. Me, I smell natural, like earth, like dirt. Keep the oils on the body where they belong.

But they don't see any of that. They keep hassling me about my dancing. And I'm not even on the dole any more! Shit, I sell enough dope, I make enough candles to get by pretty well without it. But the cops are always on my case anyway. They want to squash my dancing, they want to stop me from doing it in public. "No way," I tell them. "I dance to the rhythm of the Universe." But they just laugh when I say that like I was a retard or something.

Most nights I get ripped and go out to the field back of my rented place. Nobody bothers me there. Sam and Annie always follow and watch from a rotten log by the side of the field. I go out to dance under the stars or in the rain and fog, it doesn't matter, but I always dance alone. I start by standing perfectly still and letting the forces of the universe enter into me, like strong warm rays, all the good and beautiful forces. I give myself up to them and then when I open my eyes I see clear blue crystal everywhere like an ice palace and the shadows are smiling. And then I dance. I'm in touch then and I dance. It's a swirling, whirling dance like planets in motion, like heavenly bodies careening through space. And then I know that time doesn't exist anymore. I'm in the continuous present and death's defeated, death's not even in the picture.

Sometimes I dance all night. I lose my body and I'm just this red and living spirit floating around my field. And sometimes Sam and Annie seem to be dancing too. I see their flashing cat's eyes moving through the inky blackness and I know they're with me, that they're in touch.

When I dance in my field, everything's gone, all the bad shit, the cops, the chicks with their woodpecker ways, people trying to change you, make you small. And I'm free and large and nothing matters. My soul is a net as huge as the world and I dance it outward in larger and larger circles until I have completely covered the Universe and I am one with it. And then I'm close, man, I'm near Nirvana.

MACARONI AND CHEESE

The first time I served my family Macaroni and Cheese you might find this amusing my youngest son said What's this Mom? And pushed it away never having seen Macaroni and Cheese before let alone tasting it and not knowing that this was what poor people ate and now that his parents were no longer middle-class there would be a lot more Macaroni and Cheese dinners in his five-year-old future.

The first time I served it I cried yes I did. I served it on a Tuesday when there were no more leftovers not wanting to give up roast beef on Sundays some things are sacred. I served it carried it on a silver service tea-tray a wedding gift from Bud's great-aunt the one with the money left to cancer research and we ate it at the dining room table not the kitchen table sometimes you have to be brave.

I served a nice little salad with it too and even put the ketchup in a small cut-glass bowl because ketchup bottles on the table are dreadful. The milk too went into a pretty glass pitcher not the milk carton on the table no never the carton. But finally it was Macaroni and Cheese for dinner and I cried not boo hoo but hot squinty tears when Bud said pass the salad and pouted yes he did I could tell that hurt pouty look of his he was thinking not even a strip of bacon for godsake.

The trouble was I had never made Macaroni and Cheese before and who would I mean ever want to? I had tried a complicated recipe since I pride myself on my ability to read books do sums choose colours but what I didn't know was that this Macaroni and Cheese called for oh my god a milk sauce. And the other thing I didn't know was that with a milk sauce the milk has to be added slowly mother's told me since. How was I to know? The sauce was lumpy oh no lumpy sauce so that bits of uncooked white yes cancer-causing bleached white flour would come away in our mouths. My mouth, Bud's hurt pouty mouth, Jason Jeremy Jasper's round pink trusting mouths sucking on lumpy Macaroni and Cheese. Like sawdust said Bud it's good said Jason Jeremy. Goo said Jasper.

But Bud but Bud all Bud could do was pout sniff pout sniff then snort This looks like barf he said yes he did like barf. It's true I wailed like barf Cathy Grant serves her family barf from a silver service tea-tray cut-glass bowl pretty pitcher at the dining room table and oh what's to become of us?

I'm sorry so sorry I said Macaroni and Cheese is not ever is never ever the thing to feed an upwardly mobile white Caucasian male used to Coq au Vin Waldorf Salad Chocolate Mousse lying about all day now reading spy novels not looking for Engineer work any work. Don't be mad I should never have done it slap my hand Cathy Cathy naughty Cathy make something interesting with crackers vacuum bags kitty litter god knows I've tried hard to economize. Every magazine knows this for the truth I have them all *Chatelaine Women's Own Family Circle Western Living Ladies Digest* tasty tempting morsels for pennies for nothing. Yes there's Africa I should be thankful but the magazines don't help too many olives pimentos kiwi fruit mushroom soup min-mallows cost too much.

Nevertheless if only there was a cookbook for people like us for the newly poor rambling around in our good lives with not a cent to spend at dollar-forty-nine day not even one piece of lint. If only there was a cookbook to help those of us who used to be middle-class and who are now god help us out of work the nouveau poor and having to this whole lesser life *adjust*.

To the whole idea of budget. Can't can't can't spend like we used to. Teach old dogs new tricks like making budget a state of mind now that shopping as a way of life has cruelly ended oh it's going going gone.

Surely there must be a book about it something for smart up-to-date women like me yes I am in no need to be falsely modest. I read books do sums choose colours. Well well well. How to make hamburger casseroles for instance that don't taste like sawdust goo milk sauce don't taste like brown rice dry Third World bland. Yes I'm thankful. But show me point the way to cook healthy cook cheap cook *very* interestingly amusingly on pennies next to nothing. Make my husband smile oh make Bud smile.

I grieve yes I do for some handy little book which could point the way without getting weird getting religious. Something I could put with pride on my kitchen counter something fun. Nice pictures. Could pass around show Joan show Vicky Gail Jane Pauline the latest thing. Mother too Aunt Bee.

Some way there's got to be some way I can go on looking like Cathy Grant that Bud can go on looking like Bud Grant on the outside. Some way I can fill us up with Regular instead of Super as it were till Bud gets work does something.

Clunk. Clunk. What if he doesn't? What if finally after all it comes down to desperate Macaroni and Cheese on the best china probably sold. What if what if that's all that happens before I die some horrible lumpy milk sauce death with bits of unmelted cheese what everyone knows poor people eat. Of my own making. You make your own Macaroni and Cheese you lie in it. But never Kraft Dinner. No never some things are principles are sacred. Never ever serve that I'd sooner die not even as a joke. Oh what is to become of us?

I could heaven forbid get a job work get liberated drive a tractor sell jewelry sell clothes minimum wage. Jason Jeremy Jasper's mother a working person poor. Read books do sums choose colours for a fee by the hour? Bud forever reading Helen MacInnes John Le Carré. Furious face to the end to find out who did it.

To me? What if we start eating in our undershirts picking our teeth with matchbook covers wearing old grey wool gloves without fingers? Pick over bargain basement bins looking for something cheery yellow polyester? God forbid polyester. And Jason Jeremy Jasper turning dirty out of control eventually into mean adolescents causing social workers school counsellors juvenile judges to impose on us. Impose. Down to one car sell the house pitch a tent. No rent a welfare basement one-bedroom suite raining all the time spots on the rug.

Become less than middle-class less than average. All this life wading that wide wonderful road in middle centre between heady glitter and dirt on your face disgrace. All this life pushed off the shoulder nevertheless falling having been pushed by statistical restraint. Falling like Alice and no How-To Books in sight no good solid formulas pointing the way to be un-middle-class. How to adjust with style same on the outside no one need know how to have Bud smile again oh have Bud smile. What's to become of us? Nothing other than this whine my god we're run out of pennies run out. Of ideas there's no other way to be just the middle way no other worthwhile proper way to be no way up except lottery every way down. And terrible out. We're out. Fallen angel oh my god I'm going to start crying really cry and never stop amusing no?

Raw Material
1993

Raw Material

"Go feed Daddy," I said to my daughter Janice.

Needing something special from him, I had prepared a tray of cheeseburgers and french fries for his lunch.

Janice whined as usual—you know what nine-year-olds are like—but I said (again) that if she didn't take her responsibilities seriously then what kind of adult would she grow into?

"You have two choices," I told her, "you can either feed Daddy or you can spend the rest of your life being gnawed at by the horrible guilt which will be your due and from which there is no escape."

She fed Daddy, grumbling, mind you, but grumbling I can stand as long as they make the right decision. You can never let up with children; you must always be rigidly predictable in your responses to them. Some day I will write a book about this; child rearing is so obvious it hurts.

Janice reported back that Daddy liked his lunch but had smeared it all over his face again and that when she didn't laugh at his joke he got upset and started spitting at her.

Not for the first time did it occur to me that much of child rearing is like dog obedience: rules and expectations must be ruthlessly repeated, a monotonous chore to be sure, but so necessary in the proper handling of nine-year-olds, who are strange creatures at best—as Janice is, mostly teeth and argument and entirely without style: baseball hat, party dress, gumboots.

"Your father-daughter relationship will suffer needlessly if you fail to laugh at Daddy's jokes," I told her (again), "which means that you're going to have to clean him up or we'll never get any work done this afternoon and I'm beginning to feel desperate for a fresh idea."

We headed off towards the study at the other end of the rancher; already we could hear Daddy's shouting as he banged at his cage.

Janice kept up her toneless chatter all the while needing eye contact and "uh-huh" from me at regular intervals. She was saying something about not having adequate peer relationships because of all the time she had to spend assisting with Daddy and what kind of learning experience was it anyway if all she ever got to do was clean his cage or run the video equipment?

"I can see how you might feel," I told her. (You've got to give them some expression or they will turn into teenage time bombs.)

"However," I added, "you will soon be entering pre-adolescence and that is the time when you must start to emancipate your ego from the solipsistic concerns that now absorb you and begin to consider the welfare of the world at large. In your case, this will take the form of service to Art.

Janice replied snottily with something about my stage of life being an impossible one and that when she has children of her own she will never make them serve Art no matter how creatively important it is.

Fortunately her nattering stopped when we reached Daddy and his cage.

"Oh dear," I said when I saw him.

He was in his usual place, all right, bouncing on the recliner rocker that sits in the centre of the cage but he had smeared ketchup and mustard all over his handsome face and several bread-and-butter pickles sat atop his head.

Janice smirked nastily, a gesture that seemed to be directed at me.

"Laugh now," I said, "but where was your laughter when it was needed?" There are times when I forget that I love Janice.

She got the pail and washcloth and I unlocked the cage door. It isn't a lot of work for her, the washing of Daddy's face and tidying his cage, but enough to warrant her two-dollar-a-week allowance. Children must learn the value of money and this is why I insist that Janice save at least half of her weekly allowance for something worthwhile. I believe she's saving up for an elephant.

Daddy doesn't mind having Janice in his cage. In fact, there are times when it seems he prefers playing Crazy Eights with her to having his weekly conjugal visit from me. He reassures me, though, that his card playing with Janice is important to him, a welcome respite from the vigorous demands that my creativity places upon him. All told, we three are a happy family and this is not often the case with families who serve Art.

But it was time for me to be stern with Daddy: this food on the face routine had been hilarious six weeks back but he had been doing it every day since and it was becoming downright stale. What's the point, I reasoned, of caging up your inspiration if all it yielded was stuck records? His original action, certainly, had resulted in quite a lively story, an apt metaphor for our materialistic times, and I had been screamingly pleased with Daddy then for suggesting it but now it was time for some fresh material.

Janice, I noticed, had now changed into her visor and she and Daddy were facing each other sitting cross-legged on the cage floor in preparation for a game of cards. Janice was dealing.

"Daddy," I whispered through the bars, "you're going to have to come up with something new. I need a new line, something unexpected. A brand new angle. I'm running out of raw material."

Daddy put down his cards and, sighing, pushed at the stacks of post-modern fiction that littered the cage. I was beginning to wonder if he ever read the stuff.

"Is there anything left over from your days at the steel mill that I haven't used?" I prompted. "Some funny little thing you used to do? Some quirky little thought you used to have?"

He shook his head morosely, picked up a copy of the *New York Times Review of Books* and softly tore at its pages. I could see that he was feeling his failure.

I motioned for Janice to absent herself from the cage. Nine-year-olds do not understand nuance: you have to spell out everything for them.

"Did you look at that piece on popular culture?" I asked. "Or that new theory of Disengagement that was highlighted in *Scientific American*?

Daddy grunted.

"Nothing?"

Daddy grunted again.

"What about vanishing grizzly bears? The nuclear threat?" I cried, exasperation setting in. "Have you not had any dreams? Is there nothing left for me to use?" .

What if my inspiration is drying up, I thought with alarm. What if Daddy never yields another gem and our family business has to shut down? No more making of important fiction? Bankrupt Art? What if I have to change careers in mid-story?

Janice, meanwhile, had climbed out the study window.

Let her go, I thought. As a parent you should never take out your personal frustrations on your child; who knows what abnormal psychology they might indulge in, later on, if you do.

I had, of course, seen it coming. Daddy's off-the-wall comments, his bizarre antics (all those videos!) had become less and less frequent this past while. I had produced three volumes of short fiction based upon the inspiration I received from Daddy, but perhaps now he had nothing new to give me.

Janice climbed back in the window, pulling the garden hose behind her.

"What on earth?" I started to say just as she activated the nozzle.

A terrific gush, a quelling protester sort of gush, sprayed Daddy, the cage, the books, papers, myself.

Janice of the crazed eye manoeuvred behind the hose, all teeth and elbows, laughing maniacally.

"God is deader than thou!" she screamed.

Daddy and I, amidst the hosing, exchanged glances. "God is deader than thou!" Say it again, Janice. "God is deader than thou!"

An interesting indictment. Existential possibilities. (Juices flowing.) Children's literature? An epic poem?

But that's the joy of child rearing, I reflected, as Daddy and I wrestled the hose from Janice and locked her in the cage: you never know what they will come up with next. Fresh ideas! New angles! So important not to stifle their creative urges, to keep their little minds ticking over with wonder, excitement, awe. (Is there something to be done with elephants?)

Children have a crucial role to play in the service of Art. I've often said it's the handling that counts, it all comes down to providing them with a proper home environment: nourishing food, clear guidelines and a healthy respect for their place in the untoward scheme of things.

THE BRIGHT GYMNASIUM OF FUN

How many laughers make up a laugh track? How are laugh tracks engineered?

Is there a laugh track company? With its own building/parking lot/cafeteria? Does the laugh track company have its own stable of laughers and highly trained technicians? Are laugh track companies union shops? With shop stewards and an annual general meeting? With negotiated contracts covering such items as sick leave for laryngitis and with the right to strike for better working conditions?

Do laughers laugh at anything? At nothing? Is the mark of a good laugher one who can laugh for no reason at all, as if a switch were turned on?

Do laughers practice laughing? Sitting or standing in their living rooms/kitchens/bedrooms or on public transportation systems, do they suddenly ring out with laughter, practising the same laugh over and over until they get it right? Do professional laughers, therefore, have to carry identification on their persons at all times which will reassure startled or frightened passersby that they are indeed just practising their trade and not, in fact, mad or deranged or both?

Is there a pay scale for laughers? Are guffawers, hooters, roarers and howlers paid more for their work than are gigglers, twitters, cacklers and snigglers? Do belly laughers and shriekers command the highest fees, enough to make a decent wage? Enough to claim, in real life, the equivalent of the humorous, middle-class counterpart presented in many of the TV sitcoms they perform for?

What is real life? Is it that state of being which exists other than what is presented on television and in movies and videos? Something other than performance and posture?

Are there child laughers in special demand for childhood laugh track events such as cartoons/birthdays/tooth extractions? And what of amateur laughers? Are there how-to-laugh books developed especially for them which can be purchased at airport magazine shops/drugstores which encourage them to embrace laughing as a hobby? Are there night school courses that amateur laughers can attend in January/February/March? Tricks of the trade they can learn from practitioners who are slightly more skilled at laughing than they are? Techniques such as breath control/crescendo/decrescendo as in the training of singers and musicians? Are there laughing forms to master?

And what of those sad/abnormal souls who stubbornly refuse all merriment, all lampshade and lewd joke activity? What of them? Should there not be places/institutions/homes where they can receive treatment for their affliction? From which they can emerge, restored to rapture, and armed with tanks of nitrous oxide to declare that it is *not* better to sorrow than to laugh, it is *not* better to die than be born?

Is it true that the aging process kills off dopamine cells in the brain, that as we get older euphoria declines, and our capacity to have fun diminishes? Why there is no fool like an old fool, young fools being a dime a dozen?

Is there a market, therefore, for personal, portable laugh tracks? Small, special recording devices that we can all carry around? Attach to our persons? To enable us to laugh at our families/governments/worlds? Would illness/despair/hopelessness/anguish finally vanish as some people have suggested? Would we then all be prodded into states of chronically good moods, becoming perpetually pleased, and not tormented to death as we are now with the what-fors and whys of an absurd existence?

Would the boundaries, then, melt away between what is laughable and what is not? With everyone wearing their portable laugh tracks and laughing at everything/nothing, even in their dreams, even in love, would not the world as we know it become like one enormous California, as smooth and mild as a grapefruit? A heaven on earth? A bright gymnasium of fun?

On the other hand, in a world of stunned, uniform laughers, would there not emerge a deviant subclass, a deliberately unfunny, underground movement of anti-laughers declaring their right to misery/ bleakness/doom? Intent on the destruction of stand-up comics and gameshow hosts? Would not the cry of dadaist ecstasy be heard again, this time as "Assasinate the Laughers!" in an updated attempt to startle/ shock the smiling millions who, poised before their television screens, are laughing on cue as if possessed by some grand/homeric/universal tic?

Should not television laugh tracks be scrutinized? Do they not control the quality/frequency/duration of our laughter? Do they not disallow transcendence by rendering all experience cute? Do they not tranquilize us by rendering our laughter thin and meaningless until death do us part?

What if all the laugh track laughers went on strike? How would any of us know what is funny?

Fish

FOR VICKY HUSBAND

By day, carrying on with my fish body assembly work. By night, waking to find strangers in my bed. Last night, Mrs. Hanson and her three kids. A trial of a person.

Rip doesn't seem to mind the strangers. He just rolls over, grumbles about needing more covers, leaving me to contend.

By day, all is well. The important fish body assembly work continuing. But three nights ago, an elderly couple vacationing from Alberta. He bald and snoring, she in hairnet pondering. Maps and guidebooks spread out all over the quilt.

It's the nighttime crowds I can't stand. Whole families arguing. Some under the covers with Rip and I, others sitting on the bedside nattering.

It gets worse when I sweat because of too many people. Then I have to throw off the covers and every one starts in on me then, complaining. Many of the strangers don't like our bedroom, for instance: no proper dresser, a doorless closet, the bed merely a double. I wish I wouldn't apologize so much. *Feel so responsible.*

"Perhaps if I cleaned up the room you'd feel better," I say. "Perhaps if I slept on the floor next to the dog."

More room for Mrs. Hanson and the three kids. Mrs. Hanson slithering naked next to Rip. Mrs. Hanson breathing lullabies into Rip's dozing face.

By day I'm a person of importance. Thank heavens. With my fish body assembly work. Nearly fifty thousand so far and the numbers keep climbing. The parts from Hong Kong, duty free. That was my doing. I found the rule about location making it is permissible for a manufacturer to assemble a product on home turf thus avoiding import tax. The rule book was old but not forgotten. I take pride in that. Ferreter of antique rules.

The woman at Customs agreed, but not whole-heartedly.

"Right here on page fifteen of ENTRY REQUIREMENTS FOR PARTS FROM FOREIGN PARTS," I showed her.

She wasn't happy. They don't like to give anything away. They come to believe it's *their* rule you're tampering with.

"It's a nice rule," I told her, "one you should be proud of."

But she took it personally. That the government would be missing out on its due tax. That's dedication for you.

We all get on. Somehow. Me, I'm doing my part for the environment. Tax free. And I won't have to charge sales tax on the assembled fish bodies either because I won't be selling them. Because, in a sense, I'll be giving them away.

Rip was disappointed I didn't use my inheritance money for something more worthwhile. That's his opinion. A jazz trio, for example. I know he's always wanted one of those. Piano, bass, drums. Playing Bill Evans on demand. Actually he'd like to have Bill Evans as well. I've often hoped he'd visit us in bed but the dead can be very stubborn. So far, no show.

A Bill Evans CD wouldn't do. I suggested it.

"Too small," Rip said.

He wants to be wrapped in the live thing, ear to the electric bass speaker or sit beside the piano player and stroke his fingers while he's playing. Or crouch beneath the piano player's legs and work the peddle. Involvement. That's what Rip wants.

But I only had enough inheritance money for one of us to be involved. And after all, it's important to me that I calm things down. Quit my job at the gas station just so I could take the time.

The fish bodies are all the same size. Ten inches. Just under the legal size limit. Plastic. Overall grey in colour, made up of three sections: head, shaft, tail. Flecks of pink and blue in the plastic. Could be mistaken for a trout, a cod, or a young salmon. That's not the important part, the type. It's just so that *they can be seen to be there.*

I've always wanted to raise spirits.

Getting tired, though, with all these strangers turning up in our bed. I tell Rip about it but he just gets annoyed.

"Don't be so rigid," he says, "have a little flexibility. After all, they're not bothering you, are they? Not in any significant way? Beating you about the head or sitting on your back? Complaints about the bedroom furniture don't count. They're not actually hurting you, are they?"

Apart from Mrs. Hanson's gymnastics over Rip's body last night, I'd have to say, no, they're not.

"Well then," he says, "be like a rock in a stream, a tree in a storm. Let your turmoil flow around and away from you."

That's my Rip. He'd be a Zen Buddhist if he had the time. As it is, he's run off his feet. No wonder he sleeps through the nighttime visitors. By day, he's selling Bic pens, Eddy matches. He's got the whole territory from here to Burgoyne Bay and having the whole of anything is exhausting. So there's always someone in *his* bed. *In a manner of speaking.*

He's right, though. I make too big a deal about everything. Always have. Still.

Seven members of the Golden Eagles Day Camp the night before last. Out on an adventure sleepover with their counsellor.

Children are far too active, especially in sleep. Why I've never gone in for them. One of the campers tried to cuddle next to me, one even tried to climb into my arms. Rip just shoved them aside as if they were sleeping cats, heavy lumps. But me, I can't. I've always got to be taking charge. Half the night gone running back and forth to the fridge—juice for the campers. And then the nineteen-year-old counsellor having trouble with her boyfriend and wanting to talk. By morning I was a wreck from trying to keep everyone happy.

I can't leave well enough alone. Or in this case, bad enough alone. Doing my bit for the environmental movement. I can't stand it when people get upset. The depleting fish stocks. All the hue and cry.

My bit. Keeping the complainers happy. I have parts for one hundred and fifty thousand fish bodies. The boxes are stacked in the living room, hallway, kitchen, down the stairs to the basement. Thought of using Mini-Storage but the inheritance money is running low. If I were a midget, it would seem like a cardboard city inside our house. Towers of boxes, alleyways dark and spooky, no telling what goes on in there.

One of the campers got lost the other night on the way to the bathroom. Found her wandering terrified amongst the tail sections.

I'm especially happy about those tail sections. After all those faxes to Mr. Ni in Hong Kong.

"They've got to look like they're swimming," I faxed. "They've got to look like they're *moving in schools through the water.*"

Mr. Ni is a marvel. Even without an engineer he managed to come up with a propeller thingy that's connected to an elastic band. And he guarantees it. Either my assembled fish bodies self-propel or he'll take them back. That's business. So far, on my bathtub trials, success. Except for an occasional turn of swimming on their backs. You just pull this elastic band, the tails whirl and away they go.

I was trying to tell Mrs. Hanson about my plans last night in bed but she wasn't interested. Just wanted me to give the baby his bottle so she could get on with Rip's body rub.

The baby listened. "I will be delivering the first fifty thousand fish bodies by month's end," I told him. "I'm so excited. Rip has agreed to drive the hired truck. A dump truck. My plan is to back down the ramp at Anchor's Aweigh Marina about three in the morning. Only problem is, first I have to activate the tail sections. Otherwise, plunk, to the bottom of the deep blue sea."

Fifty thousand elastic bands snapping. I have to admit it's daunting. I'd have a nightmare about it, no doubt, if my nights weren't already so crowded. That's something. Too bad the strangers are always gone in the morning. I'm at the point where I could do with some help.

Right now what I picture before me is a string of busy, solitary days activating fish bodies. Their writhing grey forms mounting the cardboard box towers, scraping against the ceiling. Jiggling jelly. Maggot movement.

What keeps me going is *the thought*. All those upset people calmed down. Perhaps even happy. *Look there's fish in the sea!* Again. After all. In spite of.

STUDIES SHOW / EXPERTS SAY

"How much butylated hydroxyl toluene does it take to make one mutant cell?" This is the question I pose to Isobel over dinner. "One millilitre? A quarter of a teaspoon?"

"Why don't you just shoot yourself and be done with it?" Isobel screams as she packs her bags. "I'm leaving you. Sicko. Pea brain. Bag of shit. You've got gas up the ass. And I'm taking the antibiotics with me."

"You'll be sorry," I tell her. "Studies show that being cut off from friendships and family doubles a person's chance of sickness and death. Not only that," I call from my sick bed, "but experts say that it is not enough to marry someone because they make your heart pound, two people's lifestyles must come together as well. What's a nurse without a patient?"

The main thing that worries me about living alone is this: what if I should stop breathing in my sleep? Sleep Apnea. What if no one is there to roughly shake my shoulder, or if necessary, administer mouth to mouth resuscitation? What if I am found dead in my bed, a rotting cauliflower, one ghastly hand still clutching my Merck's *Manual of Diseases*?

For this reason I call up Georgina, single mother of two, my client-girlfriend from the welfare office.

I say, "About forty percent of women who separated while still in their thirties will never re-marry. Now's your chance."

*

The chest pains start on the first Sunday after Georgina moves in. We send the kids to McDonald's and spend the rest of the afternoon in Emergency. I tell them it is my fifteenth heart attack.

"Skinny guys don't get heart attacks," the intern says. "It's probably just gas."

Driving home I say to Georgina, "What does the medical profession know? They've yet to discover why I am dying."

"Everyone dies," says Georgina. "In fact the outer limit of the human lifespan remains at about one hundred and ten years and that figure hasn't changed since the beginning of recorded history."

"But you're not supposed to die in the prime of your life," I yell. "Not when you're a forty-two-year-old, white-collar welfare worker, three-bedroom home-owner secure in the middle-income profile bracket."

"You worry too much," says Georgina. "Worry wart! Next you'll be getting Herpes." Georgina is laughing.

"Very funny," I say. "Right now I'd be more worried about this pain in my lower right quadrant. I think I have a fever."

"Show me where it hurts," she says, unzipping my pants as I'm driving.

I pull over. She does the rebound test for Peritonitis, the way I taught her on our first night together. Nothing.

"Probably just a gas bubble," she says, hiking up her skirt and getting comfy.

*

Georgina lasted three weeks. She accused me of having pre-menstrual syndrome. That son of hers, Ronald, definitely has psychological problems—he called me a basket case. And I'm still recovering from the blow Curtis landed as they were leaving.

"There's a strong possibility I may be bleeding internally," I call as they head towards the waiting taxi.

"Porter Jones," Georgina shrieks from the sidewalk, "you don't need a true love, you need a fleet of ambulance attendants."

Fortunately, as a welfare worker, I am eligible for stress leave at three-quarters of my regular pay. I hate to admit to failing emotions but it's the only way I can get off work to administer to my swollen liver. My doctor has refused to see me. The things I could say about the medical profession.

*

Before long a person called Wanda follows me home from the health food store.

When I finally speak to her, as a test, I say, "I have this pain."

"People with pain almost always have something wrong in the body," she says and I am ecstatic. I know I have made a match. Wanda clinches it when she says, "I can always tell a victim of Twentieth-Century Disease. You need me."

"Okay," I say. And so to bed.

*

Wanda is an old hippie: long flowering skirt, hairy legs, several pounds of beads hanging off her neck. She has taken to preparing herbal remedies for me, teas, poultices. She gathers the herbs from her own garden and administers them to me while chanting and nodding her head towards the eastern sky, her long grey hair falling over her unhinged breasts. And furthermore, she is an excellent masseuse.

"Doctors are rip-off artists," she says.

True. True. True.

We are like-minded, Wanda and I. The things she says about the medical profession. For instance: how come, how come and how come?

How come we can land a man on the moon and we haven't yet found a cure for Agoraphobia?

How come doctors play so much golf while all over the world people are starving for adequate recreational facilities?

How come doctors get all the money while lay people like me are having to shop at the Nearly New and make a cult out of getting by with less?

She also says, "Doctors don't know dick. Anybody can see you're allergic to everything."

To this end Wanda has removed every piece of synthetic material from my house. This activity hasn't left me with much. The TV, my dishes, the kitchen table and chairs, my Dacron wall-to-wall, even the plastic toilet roll holder. All sit in a pile on the front lawn. The shower curtain. A windfall for the Sally Ann.

Not only that but she has painted the interior of my house Maalox-white, using lead-free paint. White walls, white ceilings, white floors. My house looks like the inside of a laboratory. I sleep on a white cotton futon; Wanda allows white cotton pyjamas. She vacuums dust from her naked self before visiting me from the custodial tent outside; she monitors my condition twenty-four hours a day.

She brings me cauliflower soup, the cauliflower hand-grown in the finest organic soil.

"Mineral deposits found in cauliflower are effective in treating advanced cancer of the colon," she assures me. Every day the cauliflower cure.

I spend my days wandering through the bare room in an orgy of illness. I've never felt better in my life.

*

Before long, Wanda sets up a roadside stand and is charging admission.

"Opportunity knocks," she says. "The doctors aren't the only ones to make hay out of gas."

She has called me the Bubble-Man. Sightseers now file through the flower beds and peer in at me through my curtainless, living room window. I bask in the attention, their awe-filled eyes caressing me like benevolent heat lamps. Judging from the crowds, Wanda is making a killing.

Lately she tells me that Bubble-Man T-shirts are selling like crazy. She says she is about to become President of Bubble-Man Industries, manufacturers of disease memorabilia: stool samples, vials of blood, plastic throat swabs.

"Okay," I say, "but can you tell me why I am dying? I have this pain."

"In the neck?" Wanda asks.

"All over."

"Well keep it," she says, "that pain has corporate significance."

"All right," I say, "but get me some ginger ale and some Vick's cough drops, cherry-flavoured. And fix my pillow and rub my back and bring me some magazines and bring me the thermometer. I need all the care I can get and don't you forget it."

"Not on your life," Wanda says.

All the sightseers are wearing white cotton pyjamas. Television networks are plaguing us for prime-time interviews: Bubble-Man has suddenly become an important news item and we are getting offers to do commercial endorsements.

Now everyone I have ever known is gawking at me through the living room window. In envy. Covetousness. Isobel and all her relations. Cousins I never knew I had. Former co-workers. The entire staff from the Department of Welfare. Georgina, Ronald, Curtis, their neighbours from the housing project. No one is immune. All gaze in wonder, mouthing at me through the living room window: "We never knew you'd be famous, Porter Jones. We never knew you'd be a person of importance."

Fulfillment on their faces. Tears in their eyes.

My head is spinning. I allow members of fundamentalist religious organizations to touch the hem of my pyjamas. Cripples and maniacs sit reverentially outside my window. For hours.

*

But then suddenly the doctors descend. Swarms of them are pouring over my body, taking tests, peering in my orifices. "Wanda, Wanda, this wasn't in the plan. You said doctors are the plague of the earth!"

But Wanda's nonplussed. "Things change," she says. "And studies show that businesses which use consultants wisely are more likely to flourish than those which do not. You have to be sensitive to market forces if you want to survive."

So I am charitable to the doctors, serene in my national sickness, swollen with illness-identity. I'll be a good business investment for Wanda. "A barium enema? No problem. Suck on this little metal tube? Delighted."

But when the doctors finish testing me they ponder: how come, how come and how come?

How come Porter Jones has all this attention?

How come he is lying bloated with gas on a cotton futon and is not in one of our technologically advanced medical centres?

How come a businesswoman-hippie has control of this amazing new gimmick when there are research foundations to vie for, new medical centres to be had?

The doctors buy out Wanda's interest in Bubble-Man Industries and move me to a specially sterilized Bubble-Room at their Centre.

Wanda is pleased with the settlement. "Buy low, sell high," she says as she's leaving. "Besides, I'm onto something. There's this guy, paralyzed from the waist down from eating Aspartame. He needs me."

*

My bubble has burst. After six weeks of further testing at the Centre, the doctors can find nothing wrong with me. As well, interest in me is waning; the polls show that VCRs are turning family television viewing into video campfire gatherings. This means that I am no longer being watched—I have achieved viewer saturation. My ability to command the public's attention is no longer significant.

My removal from the medical centre happened this way. I was spending my brief but halcyon days there, as usual, nursing one of my invisible, lurking tumours, or else giving interviews through the Plexiglas of my Bubble-Room when a workman burst through the door and began stripping the Saran Wrap from the walls.

"What are you doing?" I gasped. "Don't you know I'm the Bubble-Man. I have Twentieth-Century Disease. I'm allergic to EVERYTHING?"

"Got orders to re-do this room, Mac," was all he would tell me.

Within hours the Bubble-Room had been transformed to resemble the inside of a church: altar, font, cross, stained glass windows. Six hospital beds were done over to look like pews. Three nuns, three priests, all dressed in deathly black, prepared to take up residence.

"Electromagnetic clatter from millions of man-made sources is drowning out the whispers from heaven," they explained. "We're donating ourselves to medical science. Research. Soul transplants. That sort of thing. Please make way for the cameras."

In desperation I called up Georgina. "I'm being turfed out," I wailed, "thrown back to the polluting forces, my only possessions, the white pyjamas on my back, my portable heart monitor. How come, how come and how come?"

*

Today I have Diverticulitis. Yesterday it was Scabies. Last week, gritty deposits on my tibia. It's incredible the way I go on living.

I have moved in with Georgina; Isobel got the house in our divorce settlement. Because of my many illnesses I am totally unable to work. Fortunately my union at the welfare office provides me with a life-long disability pension at fifty percent of my regular wage. With the money Georgina makes as a welfare recipient, we get by pretty well, especially since we sent her kids to a group home—all those pre-adolescent hormones were giving me migraines.

It took a while to adjust to life post-Bubble but I am now, once again, at home with plague, virus and allergic reaction. Still, I am always on the lookout for a new disease which will explain my condition. Unfortunately there is not a doctor in the country who will see me.

Lately I have been troubled with Narcolepsy. I am liable to keel over in mid-sentence. It's like dropping dead, only I fall asleep instead. Nevertheless, I was able to get Georgina pregnant. I can't remember when I did this but she assures me that I am the father and not that ambulance attendant, Arnold, who is always hanging around. "For one last autograph," he winks as I plunge to the ground.

But I have fond thoughts for the child. Maybe if I can hold out through the deterioration of my sight, hearing and appetite which I know is in store for me, and the incontinence and the mental disturbance, as well. Maybe if I am still alive when the child is old enough to realize that studies show/experts say that he was born to die, that living is just a series of unexplained, uncomfortable medical conditions, occurring one after the other, sometimes all at once, perhaps then I will show him my scrapbook. Pages and pages of newspaper clippings from my Bubble-Man days, boxes full of disease souvenirs: the T-shirts and white pyjamas. It may be a distinct advantage for him to go through life with a once-famous father. On the other hand, perhaps I shouldn't influence him unduly—he'll have his own diseases to discover.

THE COMMA THREAT

I'm using up all my commas. I have a box of them sitting on my desk and I'm using them up. Well, I've given them away, as well. I gave some to my aunt to decorate her curtains; she flung handfuls of them against her drapes hoping for a Jackson Pollock effect. My son used one hundred and fifty of them for his science project on "The Way Rain Falls," using them like nails to tack down his subject. (I hated to deny him, though his use savaged my supply.) Then my mother-in-law asked to borrow at least twenty because she wanted to lengthen some sentences she was using in her Bridge game. There were some nifty bids she had in mind for her partner, she said, involving spades and top boards. She thought they'd have a real advantage if she added some commas, throwing off the competition who speak only in single words, such as "Pass" and "Hearts." And how could I say "no" to my mother-in-law who regularly lets me use her semi-colons?

But commas—those strong enough to withstand the rigours of fiction—are hard to come by. This is my problem: where to find a reliable supply. My neighbour picks up the odd bag-full for me from where she works at the school. She finds the commas fallen from text books and lying on the floor or blown in drifts beneath the blackboards. Old commas. They are from the time of ancient civilizations, from the Social Studies books, but they are prone to cracking. You put them in your sentence and before you know it, they have fallen off and a heap of them have collected at the bottom of the page. Commas from Social Studies books will just not stick so I've given up on them.

The same can be said of libraries. The whole world knows that libraries are comma-museums, the place where millions of commas have their final resting place. Just go to the section that houses ninteenth-century literature and you will be awash in commas. But, again, these are old, breakable commas and of little value. You could remove them by the wheelbarrow-full and no-one would care. In fact, you'd be doing the library staff a favour; already they are knee deep in the commas that regularly fall from the pages of Thackery and Henry James. It's appalling to realize what librarians must wade through in order to perform their book-tending duties.

The best commas come from letters of resignation, letters of termination, but these are private commas and difficult to get hold of. Still, they are likely to have the most effect in a piece because they are a substantial, finalizing sort of comma, very black in colour, and they never crack. They're the *lignum vitae* of commas, strong, and much prized if they can be found. They add a certain bleak seriousness to a piece, something I regularly covet. These commas are solid but insidious, like ticks, those burrowing ticks picked up on forest walks. The only way to get them out is to turn them slowly, counter-clockwise.

But don't tell a reader that. You start having a reader remove commas from your piece and before you know it, your words will be smashed up against each other. Panic overtakes first one sentence, then another, and then they all start rushing for the exit. The effect is domino: herds of sentences running amok through your book. Punctuation is slaughtered. It's really awful to see—all those commas strewn in the margins, leaking from the spines of books. It can have a negative effect on periods, too: it really shatters their sense of solidity. Capital letters automatically get scared and shrink. And exclamation marks! It's shocking to discover how really spineless they are. Exclamation marks will jump up and run at the slightest whiff of comma-threat; you'll find them huddled together on the back cover by the barcode. They just cannot hold their own in a sea of fluid words.

So the whole text is in jeopardy if a reader starts messing with the commas. Before you know it the sentences will have congealed into a large, black, amorphous mass and a void is created. And if you didn't realize it before now, *this* is how voids are created—by removing commas from a piece of fiction. Try removing the commas from this piece and see what happens. I won't be responsible, though, if you sink beneath the *and*s and *the*s, if you get trampled by the sudden, explosive rhythm that is unleashed, if you lose your way. Your cries for help won't be heard above the shrieks of quotation marks begging to be saved.

No, it's better if you leave the commas alone. They have a calming effect on a piece. Understand that commas are prized because they are a friend of time, slowing down the catapult, reining in the breathless. Use them decoratively,,,,,,,,,as in this sentence,,,,,,,or use them sparingly. Too many commas in a piece can cause tripping, too few, an unnecessary strain on the heart. Balance must be achieved between word-intake, contemplation, and the always-hoped-for fireworks display in the reader's mind. Commas do this by slowing down the universe just long enough for the light to shine through; they are little warriors hammering away at chaos.

And now their existence is threatened. It all started with Gertrude Stein who was not impressed with commas and felt that if you're going to pause with a thought you might just as well end it. Written advertising picked up this theme, as did the minimalists with their sleek, exquisite sentences. But, in doing so, commas were lost and, over a scant fifty-year period, the supply of good quality commas has dwindled. Sure, there are still plenty of commas around. Look in any book that specializes in adjectives, in descriptions of coastal villages, barns, and the like. But these commas are a dime a dozen, flimsy, insubstantial commas. Digest commas, temporary commas. They don't stick. Not on the page. Not in the mind. Not anywhere.

Occasionally I've gotten a small number of commas from modernist texts. They're scant but thoughtfully placed. And because they're fairly new, they maintain their shine and can really dignify a piece. But it's hard work retrieving modernist commas, like chipping paint from a window sill. You need a small chisel with a fine point, a pair of tweezers (or medical forceps) and a steady hand. It's time-consuming work, very often resulting in ripped pages. And some of those modernist commas will not budge, especially the cocky Hemingway commas which tend to fight to the death to stay on the page; you really need a washerwoman's strength to remove them. I have a set of twelve Hemingway trophy-commas which I'm saving for a special occasion. Each one is wrapped carefully in white tissue paper and set in two rows inside a black, velvet-lined case. Their procurement was the result of years of trial and error to discover the right attitude before the page: a bottle of Pernod, a canvas writing outfit, a rugged aloneness. "Comma to Momma," I might have said; it was amazing the way they surrendered.

But the supply problem persists. In fact, I've just used my last comma in this sentence after the word fact and you know what will happen now because already the periods are getting restless already the quotation marks are breathing heavy the whimpers from the text can almost be heard and it s too late to use those commas I so recklessly splashed about earlier in this piece the ones I wasted talking about comma decoration how foolish how insane to squander commas like that and now the whole text threatens to melt like jelly down a drain so do me a favour will you i ve just lost the question marks and capital letters do me a favour and send me any good quality commas you may have in your possession i don t care if they re used it doesn t matter if they re broken even half a comma would help but please before these words completely overtake me please send what ever you have my mind is going slack i beg you the words are in revolt send more commas these words won t behave they re forgetting where to place themselves and now they re runningforthehillslike

The Local Women are Performing a Traditional Dance

The local women are performing a traditional dance. Twelve of them have lined up in the parking lot outside Save-On-Foods wearing their special costumes—a loose-fitting garment made of a flowered cotton material called a *housedress*. Around their waist is tied the ceremonial apron, a square of material, also of cotton, which hangs in front of their bodies to protect the *housedress* from soap suds, grease stains, the muddy hands of grasping children. Usually the *apron* is solid white in colour but it may be pastel or checked, and sometimes it has pockets or a ruffle around the edge. It all depends on which locale the women are from. Urban women are known for canvas *aprons* in solid colours, women of the suburbs for nostalgia *aprons* trimmed with lace. Pay close attention: the *apron* of former times was used (metaphorically) to tie the women to something called *domesticity*, a state of hominess created by them for men and for children.

The dancing women wear dark red lipstick, their faces are smudged with pastry flour and from their hands swing *cast iron frying pans*. On their feet are the authentic *fuzzy pink slippers* of the dance and though difficult to imagine, these slippers have been solemnly passed down from one generation of dancer to the next. They are made of acrylic—a petroleum by-product which will last for ever. The dancers' heads are covered with *curlers*, three-inch metal tubes around which strands of hair are wound and affixed to the head with steel pins called *bobby pins*. These *curlers* complete the traditional dress.

Now watch as the women dance. Those strings of single-family dwellings, plastic laundry baskets, dogs, cats, sectional sofas and six-month-old babies which are attached to the yellow polypropylene cord trailing from their right ankles are called *domestic paraphernalia.* They form part of the complicated twirling and hopping movement of the dance. Each dancer must spin in a circle, moving at such a rate as to lift the cord off the ground. She will then hop over the spinning cord at least once with each rotation. Two hops are sensational. Three—nothing less than sublime.

The more *domestic paraphernalia* trailing from the right leg of a dancer, the more prestige a dancer will have. This is because a long, heavy line of goods will be harder to spin and hop over than a shorter one. Fatigue is a problem, as is tripping because as the dancer spins she must jump higher and higher. Only the best dancers can sustain the dance.

The traditional dance of women is a frantic dance and the accompanying music must reflect this frenzy. Circus music meant for jugglers and acrobats is good. Hurried up versions of "Entrance of the Gladiators" or "The Flight of the Bumble Bee" are also used. So is "The One Minute Symphony"—repeated endlessly.

Now you know why the women's traditional dance is performed in an empty parking lot—the hazard factor—the essential ingredient of all good dances, that brush with death. Any minute now a house could be loosened from the strings of *domestic paraphernalia* and be hurled into the spectators. Hence the expression: *raining cats and dogs.* So stand back. As a member of the crowd you've got to be careful, keep your head down, and be aware of the exits.

When the women perform their traditional dance the effect can be dizzying. Twirling, stomping, shouting, the momentum quickens, the paraphernalia spins. Whole city blocks have been toppled by flying debris. Sometimes the dancers themselves take flight, riding their washing machines and garbage cans high over the heads of the gasping spectators. Once Delores Delmonte, that famous, furious solo dancer unleashed a shopping mall. A terrible, wonderful sight.

This group we're watching now is particularly fine, especially that woman, third from the left, the one in the pink-and-blue-check *housedress*. She's managed to string a good six hundred metres of domesticity behind her. Even a small Bank—no wait, there's more. Several institutions as well—a hospital, a school, a television station. My god, she's spinning her cord two feet off the ground. An inspiration! And her jumps! Look at those jumps. Two! Three! There's a fourth! And she's still upright. Incredible. But hold on. That school is coming loose. There it goes, yes, it's beginning to rise. A magnificent ascent.

And those children. Look what's happening to those children: shaken from their classrooms along with their desks, books, blackboards, teachers. Sprinkling over the crowd like confetti.

Bravo!

Bravo!

Score

My husband of eighteen years announced he was going back to his first wife. He'd been married to her for two years twenty years ago and brought many stories of hating her to our marriage. I loved those stories. One time she flung herself screaming onto the hood of his car. Once, in a fit of anger, she smashed his tropical fish tank. Fifteen Siamese Fighting Fish, seven Zebras, two Tri-coloured Sharks flopping for air on the wall-to-wall Berber.

But your first wife? I asked him. Why?

Real estate, he said.

The first wife had become part of our family's history but I wasn't eager for her to take over the here and now. Our kids called her Boo Boo. I called her Boo Hoo, though her real name was Charlene. She was famous for crying.

Tell me again, I said. Why real estate?

She makes a lot of money, my husband said.

I tried a thing or two to change his mind. While I might not be making bags of money thinking about this wily world, I do on occasion write a clever story. I tried sitting at my desk naked from the waist down, pencil in hand. No interest. I invented some zappy Erma Bombeck thoughts, put them inside a cartoon bubble and attached the bubble to his mind on a string. Ho hum.

I tried keeping score for him. I kept score anywhere I could. On the fridge door in black marker I wrote: My Life l8 – Her Life 2. He didn't find it funny. I arranged his Cheerios on a plate to read: Dead

Tropical Fish 24 – Current Live Household Pets 4. On his Father's Day wrapping paper I scrawled: Our Children 2 – Her Children 0. But his heart was thrusting elsewhere.

Tell us about the time crazy old Boo Boo stayed in the cherry tree for three days and cried because you forgot her birthday. This from our youngest. Tell us about the time she slugged you in the bar. The time she spiked your tea with Ex-Lax. The time she went on your job interview and did all the talking to make sure you got the job. Stories better than Archie. I saw my mistake. On the front door with red crayon I wrote: Boo Hoo Nostalgia Tales 23 – Resident Adult Female's Neo-Neurotic Tales of Life & Laughter 5,292.

Then I cleaned the fridge. My husband said, Twice in eighteen years is not a good score. Our son said, It looks like you won't be making it to the play-offs.

As a tribute to the extra mile I was running on behalf of the family, I abandoned books on philosophy and took up a new kind of reading. I got a book on dances; I'd heard it takes two to tango. A book on archaeology, leaving no stone unturned. A book about growing grass over the septic tank, with special instructions for laughing at all costs. I was looking for a doorway into not caring.

Finally I asked my husband that pearl of a question: What can she give you that I ... ?

Small kitchen appliances, he said, then listed them off: an electric popcorn maker, a toaster oven, an ice-cream machine, three different models of blender, a food processor, an electric can opener, an electric knife, a hand-held electric mixer, an old-fashioned electric mixer with three sizes of bowls that fit into each other, a yogurt maker, an electric juicer, a bread maker, five different kinds of coffee makers, a singing kettle, an electric kettle, a small microwave oven for the family room.

Big deal, I said. What else?

History, he said, getting to the science of the matter.

History? I asked. What about the time she cleaned up in the divorce settlement? Remember what a maniac she was? All you got was the idiot dog and the hat stand.

Exactly, he said. Once-upon-a-time. I'm sick of the present.

You want history? I said. Well, remember this. Then I burned down the house.

Standing before the charred and smoking elbows of two-by-fours which had once been our three bedroom split-level on a quiet cul-de-sac, my husband looked at me with new interest.

Our son said, remember the time Mom burned down the house because Dad was going back to Boo Boo. Even though it happened only an hour ago. Our daughter said, I loved it when Mom had all that ash on her face. She looked like something out of *Star Wars*. There was pride in their voices.

My husband said, Okay, you win. I'll settle for a two-hole toaster with a special slot for toasting English muffins.

We moved to a motel. Our son hung a victory banner over the doorway to room 203. It read: HISTORY RULES.

For a while I didn't mind running the history-making department; I believed it was my duty as a parent, as a fully participating member of the community. And, I reasoned, when you've got history you've got time at your back—it doesn't get a chance to over take you. You can sit on a lawn chair and not worry about time passing you by. You can dangle your feet over the edge of your existence, lean on fence-posts if you can find one, drum your fingers monotonously on card-board tables. I can see the sense of this, the beauty of this. But there's history and there's history.

I packed my bags and moved next door to room 205. A day later I heard our daughter say, remember the time Mom said that history is a whole world of meanings and not just memorable events strung out in a hopscotch line? I liked it when she climbed onto the motel roof with the megaphone, the way the crowd gathered like a threatening storm, and the firemen and the sirens.

I had done none of these things. It looked like my daughter was well on her way to creating a remember-the-time world of her own.

But my husband?

I called up Boo Hoo. He's all yours, I told her.

Who? she said. Never heard of him.

The Children Do Not Yet Know

The children do not yet know what goes on beneath the bedsheets. We, of course, visit there regularly because that is where the airport is and, as you get older, the flights you can take there become more and more appealing.

Right now, the children believe that something titillating goes on beneath the bedsheets, although they don't know this for sure. Grave gropings, perhaps, or the warm sponge of torsos, buttocks and breasts.

We do not plan, as yet, to tell the children about the airport because we feel that they should wait their turn. After all, they have a fair bit of youth ahead of them and won't be interested in flight until they are done tramping around in the awkward mud of concrete things: mortgages, income tax returns and the like.

Our friends feel the same way as we do. It's a favourite topic with us at our backyard barbecues: when to tell the children about the airport. We are all in favour of waiting until they are fully adult and then presenting the airport to them as a kind of consolation prize for responsible, middle-class living.

We first found the way to the airport by accident, under my husband's pillow, and a welcome discovery it was. I banged my head on it—my husband trying to squeeze new life out of an old situation—and, yes, I would have to say that since we have found the airport, a new intensity has entered into our marriage.

We spent weeks just trying to pry open the solid oak door (much grunting, much straining) and then several more clearing the descending wooden staircase of debris and repairing loose planks.

When we finally reached the airport we were enchanted. A white-washed tarmac stretching for miles toward a distant horizon, a flat mega-canvas dotted here and there with the shining forms of silver aircraft. Overhead, a cloudless sky. And not another person in sight. We immediately ran in different directions, my husband to a B-52 Bomber and I to a sweet, twin-engined Cessna with wings decorated to look like the wings of a butterfly, yellow and orange, much like the fabric design on our patio furniture.

The best flights, we have since found, are night flights, although we have been known to slip down for a quick one on a hot, sleepy afternoon.

Very often the children will be out building something in the back yard, a stadium, say, out of old boards and upturned flower pots or a vast city-complex out of empty margarine containers, cookie boxes and G.I. Joe tanks. I might be in the kitchen doing up the lunch dishes and my husband, standing at the kitchen window looking out at our children.

He might say to me very quietly, "Feel like a short flight, Barbara?" and I, smiling coyly and glancing toward the window, might say, "Well, Raymond, if you think there's time ... "

We have many flights to choose from. There's the Run Away From Home Flight, The Adulterous Affair with Gummy Genitalia Flight, The Chorus Line and the Lonely Businessman Flight, The Family Flight, The Rescue Flight (a heaving sea of red jello) and The Vampire with the Enormous Penis Flight. These are some of our favourites.

Our friends like to visit our airport and we like to visit theirs. We have a great many friends and they are all, like us, unremarkable in the general silence of things. Many times when I drive through the city and see the crowds of unremarkable people going about their business, I wonder what it is that keeps us all like-minded. TV was my first thought but now I know it to be the airport. Having an airport beneath our bedsheets is the best kept secret of unremarkable people.

My husband continues to be quite definite about waiting to tell the children about the airport. Every time he returns from a flight, he tells me this. You see, he spends a great many hours away from his sales job sitting in the corner of our living room reading books on magic to impress the children but they remain unimpressed by the fantastic. Faeries, splendid castles, secret doors are a solid bore to them; they want the full dose of palpable reality. Fantastic to our children is the existence of the San Francisco Giants, or the black garbage truck that prowls our street on Mondays, or the World Atlas with its peacock display of nation flags in the index, or the thrill of commerce—having their own garage sales. It is only unremarkable, middle-aged adults like us who are lured by the fantastic: you spend half your life trying to dominate the physical world and the rest of it trying to forget what you know.

So we are very happy to have found our airport. And before long, when our children have become unremarkable adults themselves, they will be able to experience the airport, too. At that time, a final mystery for them will be solved. They will understand why, for all these years, their father and I have been so eager to go to bed in the evenings. Why we must have our Ovaltine at nine. Why our reading material must be arranged on the bedside table just so. Why the pillows must be plumped and the feather quilt made smooth to resemble a white-washed tarmac. These are all the preparations which my husband and I regularly take so that at midnight, if all is quiet in the household, we can join hands and descend the long, wooden staircase to our airport and the purring F-117 Stealth Bomber that awaits us there.

ALTERED STATEMENTS
1995

THUNDER SHOWERS IN BANGKOK

*Sitting on these front steps. Two drunks go by saying my name. Hello,
you two, hello.*

They were all there, all the important ones, on the cover of the
final issue: Mina Holland, George Van, Howard Curtail. The three of
them looking solemn, standing full-faced before the camera, posed on
a freeway overpass. Cars and trucks behind them, indistinct, a blur,
a streak of grey because of the slow exposure. And only the poets in
focus, as if they'd stepped out of time, walked away from the murky
world. The photograph in black and white, the magazine title and
their names printed in red.

I was living in a third-floor room then, on the corner of Railway
and Fourth. People from the old days dropping by to read their
works. One we particularly admired, though his output was small:
John Savage, or Savage John as he called himself then. We knew him
for his warmth and accessibility but that was only one extreme. His
work was marked by bleakness and we spent many hours talking of
this, how this could be so. I felt that the bleakness was true and said
how we are always on the edge and that this is the truest reality—
knowing as much about this life as we are able to bear. After that we
become giddy and drunk and must have the necessary moments of
forgetfulness. This thought became the theme of the final issue, the
preface, a quote from Lorca: *Life is laughter amidst a rosary of deaths.*

Years later John Savage was found dead on the 401, the top of his
head shaved off but clutching that last important work. He'd had a
part-time job washing down the freeway at night. Tough work but
possessing the right amount of scrab. Scrabbing was what we were

93

about—the low-lying, lizard-crawling belly living where we found our poems. The diving deeply, the geyser quest. And we put out this journal whenever we could. *Thunder Showers in Bangkok*, we called it, because that was right too.

In those days we'd mine the junk heaps of this miserable city, finding our poems in the grimiest of places. Creating our jewels from the trash of the age. At times we'd read in the lobby of the public library for the street people and the mentally confused who gathered there for the warmth. Or hold poetry festivals in church basements where maybe three or four strangers would attend.

Little by little, we witnessed the death of the literary age.

And now?

Cities are dying for lack of what we were able to say.

Electronic wizardry is everything.

And we find ourselves committed to very small acts, hoping to find a manageable content, some link, some rope to swing on. Reduced to servicing our intense inverted passions because out there is so unknowable.

Ordinary reality is not all there is and, to put it bluntly, is something of a bore. Breton said that, or maybe it was Blake. It doesn't matter. This is the beginning of the twenty-first century and we like to mix things up, everything from all the times, frothing together in a crazy late life stew. And so I've arrived on these steps where I spend my days watching the drunks go by. Didn't use to be so many drunks, now they're going by all the time. The eternally stunned, the eternally confused. And I'm living in slow time. Even without a watch I know the hour, the day, almost to where the moment is tethered. The rest of the world is beyond me, an indistinct blur, in nanosecond time.

This work of enlarging the orb. I've spent my life at it.

As my farewell to the world I'll compose an engaging little partita set in a minor mode. Composed while still scrabbing in the slow time of existence. As a tribute to those who have gone before me, to those who are no more. I've learned this much: to be human now is to partake of a cult existence.

Two drunks go by saying my name. Hello, you two, hello.

Don't bother sketching in a past for me, the two-step to this final step. That's sociology. Cause and effect. That's all about redemption. I've become part of an equation that takes six billion particles to balance. In other words, I have my place. Call it betwixt. There's a word—between two states. The twin pillars. The doorway to light guarded by two miserable hounds.

The last copies of *Thunder Showers in Bangkok* are stacked beside my bed. Buried treasure in a handful of words.

There's a tour bus leaving every half hour from the station. You won't want to miss it. Word has it that tonight the children will be violating the city. Some as young as eight, none older than fifteen. Several of their crowd are supposed to be hanged in Memorial Park. Something to do with a bushfire of bad feeling.

ALICE & STEIN

That first while Stein carried her bride around Paris in a white canvas bag. I will have the introductions slow, she said, only a few will meet her.

Those fortunate few would join them for dinner in the Louvre where a wooden table had been set up in the foyer beneath Michelangelo's sculpture of David. Stein would heave the canvas bag onto the table. Inside was tiny Alice Toklas.

My bride, said Stein, my beautiful, beautiful bride, dark and gnarly as a walnut. She lifted Alice Toklas gently by the belly and placed her on a chair.

Don't put me near the window, Alice screamed, you know how I hate a view!

*

Stein excelled at performing on stage. Any opportunity and she'd build a platform, often with boards and nails. She'd build one anywhere. Showing up at a former friend's house, after years and years, she'd start building a platform in the backyard, hauling the two-by-fours for the foundation herself, adding wide planks as needed. The friend's children mistaking her for a stranger, this heavyset, short woman with the smooth, tanned skin and the hook nose, her hair cut like a man's, like Caesar's. No, you couldn't call her handsome—intriguing perhaps, a little frightening. But what things she knew! What secrets she told from her stage!

Stein wrote for twenty minutes each day. You can write a lot of books if you do that, she said. She also said: No one cares if you don't write.

But mostly Stein thought: About how to end the nineteenth century ... How to pull the world of literature into the twentieth century ... How to make a composition of language ... How to make words stay on the page composed ...

Everything I have done has been influenced by Cézanne and Flaubert, she said.

Tramping over the hills and roadways of southern France, wandering through the streets of Paris in search of building materials for her many platforms. Thinking: One human being is as important as another ... a blade of grass has the same value as a tree ... in composition, all words have the same value.

One or other of her dogs as companion, her two great Standard Poodles, Basket and Basket 2.

She said: I like a thing simple but it must be simple through complication.

She said: Biography is the true form of the twentieth century.

*

Things As They Are ... Potomac ... The Making of Americans ...

*

Alice kept house. Her job: sweeping up the unknown. Not a leisurely sweeping, but a rushed, hurried sweeping. There's only so much time! she'd cry, and so much dust!

The more she swept, the more she uncovered. She swept up bucketfuls of dirt, clumps of mud, dust as plentiful as sand. Once she unearthed an unpublished book of poems by Rimbaud. The first page, first sentence reading: Wants! Those gnarly fingers from Hell!

Stein dismissed the book saying: Too much passion, too many birds flying off the page.

*

One time Stein roped together some logs in a harbour, and then climbed aboard. Another platform. This was in Marseilles. When no one paid attention, she suspended a cable 100 feet from a bridge, attached the cable to the back of her suit jacket, and hung herself from the bridge like a spider. This scared Alice so much she immediately began publishing Stein's work herself.

*

Geography and Plays ... Ladies Voices ... Pink Melon Joy ... If You Had Three Husbands ... Advertisements ... Scenes, Actions and Dispositions of Relations and Positions ... A Long Gay Book ...

*

In the evenings Stein sat in their Paris studio beneath her portrait done by Picasso and talked to the artists, writers, and musicians who dropped by. The studio: one room in a four-room apartment at 27 rue de Fleurus. Paintings on every wall, each above another, all the way to the ceiling. Stein's studio platform: a low chair, the fabric designed by Picasso, hand-stitched by Alice.

Everyone came by, especially writers. The French poet, Cocteau. The Americans—Fitzgerald, William Carlos Williams, Hemingway, Dos Passos. All wanted her acknowledgement, her blessing. She said to Hemingway: Remarks are not literature. Advised him to quit the newspaper business and get on with *The Sun Also Rises*. Later, she said he failed as a novelist because he couldn't handle time; his training in journalism had ruined him for art.

The worst thing Stein could say to you was that she wasn't interested in your work.

The worst thing Alice could do to you was not invite you back.

Everyone remembered Stein's laugh: deep, rich, a contralto's voice.

Alice never laughed; she was too busy tending guests, shopping at the market. Stein can laugh for us both, she once said in an interview: Laughing is Stein's domain; silence and reverie are mine.

*

Tender Buttons ... Susie Asado ... A Movie ... .A Saint In Seven ... Portrait of Mabel Dodge ...

*

Alice dusted the pictures. The Picassos, Matisses, Cézannes, Renoirs. The Grecos, Toulouse-Lautrecs, Daumiers, and a moderate-sized Gauguin.

She was small, exotically dark, wore gypsy rings and tapestry shawls. She was famous for her recipes; she had thousands of them—for eggs, for veal. Specializing in sauces made of butter, egg yolks, sugar, vermouth.

She said she had only met three real geniuses in her life: Picasso; Alfred North Whitehead; and Stein. She did not say how she knew they were geniuses.

The wives of geniuses, near-geniuses, and might-be-geniuses that I have sat with! she said.

In her kitchen the artists' wives were served their tea.

Chinese tea, lightly fragranced.

*

Stein wrote in longhand. Alice organized and typed the manuscripts, first on a small French portable, then on a sturdy Smith Premier. She suppressed publication of a first novel because it was about a love affair Stein had had with another woman.

After this novel, Stein kept passion strictly out of art. It does not belong there directly, she said. But it's there, oh yes, it's there, early on, and later it's there: anger, joy. She had her romantic moments. ("Lifting Belly" was a love song.) In fact, she had a "Romantic Period" during the twenties. This was after her "Spanish Period," and before the later and more accessible "Elucidation Period."

Alice's periods were of a sensual nature: her "Egyptian Head Dress Period," her "Blue Glass Bead Period," her "White Wine With Breakfast Period." And for the lonely twenty years she served as a widow after Stein's death, her "Bleak Letter Writing Period."

*

The summers in the south of France, the Paris studio. Stein's Model T. The trips to Spain. Years of this. Stein and Alice living on an allowance from Stein's brother Leo. Their ambulance work in France during the First World War. Their many friends amongst the GIs. Stein's few supporters; her many platforms falling into disrepair. The sale of paintings to help pay the rent, publish the books.

*

Occasionally Stein would succumb to the public ridicule, the constant rejection of her work. Alice would find her, mid-afternoon, collapsed on the studio couch, lying fetally, uncomfortably on her side. For a heavy woman, looking very small.

Anything you create you want to exist, she told Alice. Being in print is how my creations live. They are trying to destroy my children.

Alice told her: There's a vacant lot filled with wooden planks down on the rue de Christine and it's a fine day for building a platform.

*

Summer, 1926, the south of France. Stein took Alice by the hand. Led her to a meadow where they made love. All afternoon they lay on the grass, hearing nothing but the wind, the murmur of bees, the rush of low flying birds. Alice was nervous lest they be found in so revealing a situation. But Stein was calm, smiling up at the wide blue sky, Alice's head on her lap. My wife, Stein whispered, my beautiful, beautiful wife.

That enormous presence with the dainty hands, the small neat head. Alice called her Baby.

*

An Acquaintance With Description ... Four Saints in Three Acts ... Lucy Church Amiably ... A Valentine to Sherwood Anderson ...

*

Each October, for forty years, they celebrated their anniversary by taking tea in Montmartre. Then a stroll through the Luxembourg Gardens.

Alice always gave Stein a gift, something she had made herself— a hat, gloves, silk-lined underwear. Or a brooch. Alice was fond of amber and things caught in glass—feathers, stones, lace.

On their anniversary, Stein presented Alice with a New Work, untyped: *Wars I Have Seen ... Everybody's Autobiography ... A Waterfall and A Piano ...* Written on the sly, without Alice's knowledge. The weeks leading up to the presentation filled with excitement, anticipation, joy.

Stein's pet name for Alice was Pussy.

*

*Grant or Rutherford B. Hayes ... Page IX ... The Superstitions of Fred
Anneday, Annday, Anday; A Novel of Real Life ... Ida ... Is Dead ...
The Autobiography of Alice B. Toklas ... How Writing is Written ...*

*

The triumphant American tour in 1934. Stein was famous now, after
publishing *The Autobiography of Alice B. Toklas* in 1932. The headlines said: GERTY GERTY STEIN IS BACK HOME HOME BACK. She'd been
away for thirty years. Travelling first class with her wife, Alice, aboard
the *SS Champlain*, they had flowers in their cabin from the Duchesse
de Clermont-Tonnerre, were asked to dine at the Captain's table but
declined. A small child whom they met onboard is rumoured to have
said that she liked the man, but why did the lady have a moustache?
In New York they found themselves bombarded by reporters and
cameramen. Stein loved the attention. When a reporter asked, Miss
Stein, why don't you write the way you talk?, Stein replied, Why don't
you read the way I write?

For the trip Alice made Stein a leather case in which to carry her
lecture notes. Also a copy of a hat that belonged to Louis XIII. There's
a picture of them taken on the deck of the *Champlain*. Stein is
wearing this hat, a somewhat unremarkable hat, close fitting with a
small brim. In the picture, Alice is shown carrying both hers and
Stein's handbags; she has a defiant look on her face. And, yes, you
can see her moustache.

*

*I Came and Here I am ... Answers to the Partisan Review ... The New
Hope in Our "Sad Young Men" ... Off We All Went to See Germany ...
All About Money ...*

*

In the mornings, if it was summer, Alice gathered strawberries for Stein's breakfast. From the market if they were in Paris, or from the garden beside their country home. (Stein never arose before noon.)

Then, together at the breakfast table: a bowl of berries followed by eggs Benedict, fresh bread and strong coffee. Sun through the window; rays of sunlight shining on the table, on their bent heads, like a still life. A vase of flowers, the morning papers. A breeze through the open window. And Stein and Alice talking quietly, their intimacy with words. The plans for the day. A walk, perhaps, a manuscript to type.

They spoke to each other in perfect tenses, abhorring adverbs, weaving their profound repetitions, never saying the same thing twice, a living speech.

About Stein's perfect present, her friend, Bernard Fay, had said: Her life and her work are as pleasant as a cold bath in the heat of summer.

*

Stein said: Dead is dead. Anyone is living who has not come to be dead.

Alice said: Baby was my life.

KRISTMAS KRAFT

I heard about this cute Christmas gift idea that you can make at home—your own Kraft nativity scene, colourful too, and mmm-mmm yummy.

First hollow out a three pound brick of your favourite luncheon meat so that it resembles a stable and so that you, looking down through its roof, look like an angel. Then put your stable onto a cookie sheet and surround it with shredded coconut. This is the hay. Next stick four tooth picks into four wieners and stand them up. Top each wiener with a Kraft green olive. These are the cattle. For Mary, top an upright cocktail wiener with a Mini-Mallow and use strands of coconut for her hair. A hollowed out Maxi-Mallow will do for the manger and the infant Jesus will be a cocktail wiener wrapped in a Kraft Cheese single. Surround the table and the hay with Miracle Whip and shredded Velveeta Cheese.

Take a picture.

Then place your Kraft nativity scene in a three hundred and seventy-five degree oven for forty-five minutes. Serve when friends drop over on Boxing Day or use as a festive centrepiece, a Merry Christmas gift from Mom in the kitchen, that happy lady, that wise shopper.

On Holiday with Giants

Our children are larger than us. They carry us about on their huge backs like packsacks, you on the boy, I on the girl. Riding them through the city streets in search of playmates it's evident that other parents are being carried about in a similar way; some are even slung on their children's hips like bags of groceries, some ride anxiously on fat shoulders. Then we are set down in designated areas for drink and conversation, dozens of parents gathered together for worried viewing of the park across the way; the children are playing their fearsome games there with baseballs the size of pumpkins, and bats sturdy enough to support a house. Grandparents, no bigger than dolls, sit amongst us nodding quietly to one another: Ah, the wisdom of the world!

At night it's back to the hotel room. You and I in a corner of the room sharing a single mattress on the floor. The children each with a king-sized bed arranged before the TV set where they watch game shows and eat peanuts—the shells rising in mountains from the floor. The room growing smaller by the minute. The children growing larger and larger.

During the night the room heats up like an incubator. But the children don't notice. They sleep with massive fists thrust in their pink gaping mouths. When our daughter laughs and tosses in her sleep her roundness bruises the hotel walls. At three A.M. our son cries out in a man's voice: Barricade the door, the troops are coming! His size twelve feet flailing against the hotel quilt.

We, on the floor, sweat and lose moisture, shrivel a little more, dry out. Our lotions of little help. Our lovemaking of little help. We keep reducing in volume. Peanut shells spill onto our mattress. On the way to the bathroom we wade through a clutter of pop cans and pizza cartons, track shoes, comics.

Regarding these sleeping giants, we realize it's too late not to have had them. The die has been cast. Inexplicably, our pride in them remains.

GREEN PLASTIC BUDDHA

How to keep going considering the arbitrary nature of the world. That's my problem. I look for signs. Yesterday I found a pen on Beacon Avenue outside Cornish's Book and Stationery. A white Bic pen taped over with Dennison Pres-A-Ply. The writing on it said, "My Science Project Sucks Shit." Surely, a message from the spheres.

I'm always bargaining with chance. It's an addiction like teenage masturbation, you're always promising yourself that this is the last time. If I empty the sink of water before the kettle boils … If I make it to the stop sign before that man crosses the street … Grovelling for trivial favours. I can't help fiddling with the inevitable.

That time I traded Christmas crackers with my aunt, it was a mix-up, she sat at my place so I sat at hers. Then we opened the crackers. She got the skull and crossbones key chain, I got the green plastic Buddha, though both our paper hats were blue. Eight months later she died. It didn't matter that she was an old woman. What mattered was that she got the sign, not me.

Today we talked about renewing the mortgage on the house and you said it depresses you to think of a twenty-five year amortization rate because in twenty-five years you'll be dead. You're sure of it while with each birthday I've come to place my age at exactly half of what I'll be when I die and I keep on dying older and older. When I wait for our daughter after school I count the seconds until I see her come out of the portable. I make myself count slowly, calculating how many years I've got left. If it's a good day I make it to forty-six but most days I cheat, pretend I haven't seen her running behind a group of kids at count fifteen or twenty-three. Eternity is not something I'm after.

I use the Bic pen I found on Beacon Avenue to do accounting. It's not by chance that when I'm not working with words, I work with numbers. There's something solemn about movement in a closed system. Those rows and columns of quiet black numbers have a beauty all their own. I'm always surprised at which numbers dominate the day. Sometimes it's fours and sixes, sometimes it's eights, nines and twos, running like pure, emotionless currents through the page. Each story, each piece of fiction I write is an attempt to defer eternity and we all know what eternity is: it's the silence beyond time, it's that place where we have nothing to cling to.

The green plastic Buddha sits on my desk, scotch-taped to a rock you brought back from the beach, its gaping, idiot face still saving me from nothing.

VACATION TIME

Each summer during the two weeks of vacation time goldfish flee their bowls to build dazzling orange nests in trees. Monkeys, lions and snakes trade places with accountants, lawyers, and priests, holidaying in another kind of zoo. Free birds fly voluntarily into cages allowing their rarer brothers a two-week dose of the sky. All the hard-working ants, red and black, get two weeks off to loaf on the beach. Worms crawl out of their dirty holes to hang like brown tinsel from the eaves of churches.

During the two weeks of vacation time every wronged animal is avenged: gangs of domestic cats and kamikaze budgies rampage the streets in search of juvenile delinquents; a committee of gerbils and hamsters makes plans for the eradication of small boys; angry butterflies work round the clock sharpening their specimen daggers; pet turtles grow temporarily huge commanding their owners to languish in slimy tanks on the front lawn—two weeks go by and they don't feed them or change the water.

During vacation time, old women watch in horror as their pet terriers turn into porcelain dogs, as their china figurines come leeringly alive—girls with parasols, boys with fishing poles—to run off for two weeks of fragile sex in a place far away from glass cabinets.

There is a Competition for the Hearts and Minds of the People

1. Earth, Air, Fire, Water

EARTH

He is calling for an end to the fighting and three days later the government strike heats up and one man was wrestled to the ground. And the cupboard is bare and the union was blamed and we sought to confront the deficit and it could be law within a few days. And we continue to crawl out of the recession and strong growth in the manufacturing sector is forecast and guidelines were laid down and tougher guidelines were laid down in July. And he was not available for comment. And a former justice minister has died and the service sector is suffering. They were stopped by police and their dogs at the border. They are planning to file a complaint and have released their plans. They promise to regain the public interest. A major announcement will come tomorrow and he is keeping his options open and he is convinced he has to do something and no details were released.

AIR

He's here to open a trade office and a moderate earthquake shook the city last night and canned goods from supermarket shelves fell onto supermarket aisles. A makeshift morgue has been set up in a football field and the scientists are worried. And the women are worried about take-it-or-leave-it propositions. A delegation was told they should listen to the people but he warns of major stumbling blocks. He says real reasons were sought and key proposals are missing. A major reconstruction program has been set up and a similar plan was put on hold four years ago. He's meeting with the strongest resistance. The women say the process has completely retreated behind closed doors and he says he may not be able to maintain his headquarters and the peacekeepers are nervous. The rescuers are searching through the rubble. A flock of whooping cranes is to be released in Florida next month.

FIRE

He still refuses to resign and the protesters have been ordered to disperse. Police will use tear gas if necessary. They're bracing for a bad news budget and thousands have been left homeless. Most of the key suspects avoided capture by committing suicide and the coroner's report is not optimistic. He says he's no fan of the current round of talks; the most critical answers to the most critical questions are still unresolved. Earlier police shot into crowds of protesters. A crowd throwing stones blocked the visit. They fired a warning shot across the bow of the conference. They do not want a confrontation with their giant neighbour. Everyone believes he is behind the violent demonstrations. They say he has psychiatric problems but they don't believe he is dangerous. One of the workers says he fears for his life.

WATER

There is a competition for the hearts and minds of the people. It began last week and continues despite stiff opposition. Representatives from the warring factions have been arguing over the plan. The lines are being drawn, the promises given. The proposals are being looked at. He says the victims must take action and a prosperity council is being called for but may be delayed. So far fifty managers from four departments say they'll come to the table. Millions of taxpayers are baffled and the officials insist that there is nothing wrong. More then a million people risk starvation *this winter. The party manipulated public fears and now there are concerns. A nicotine by-product has seeped into the nation's drinking supply. And a new rule will be announced tomorrow. He says today's meeting wasn't easy to organize, special deals had to be arranged and he is clearly dissatisfied with the results. There is a void and it needs to be filled. People are dying every day. The ministry says they will look into the matter. There are too many discrepancies in the story. It's possible there are people out there who have information.*

2. ALTERED STATEMENTS

THE DEPARTMENT OF HOPE

If the public has been confused again, we're sorry. We know it happens each morning at daybreak with the unearthing of the Image Store and, like most citizens, we're concerned with the eruption of unsanctioned images which can appear at that time, particularly those images of sickness and death, and of phantom landscapes emitting a strange and haunting beauty. Our early morning radio newscasts which break into sleep have been designed to subvert these rebel images and we urge citizens to make use of them.

We at the Department understand your distress but again remind you that it is dangerous to indulge in independent dreaming and fantasizing or in exotic reading of any kind. Indeed, we actively discourage these seditious practices. Our aim at the Department is the eradication of the unknown and we're confident that the citizenry endorses this goal.

A machine which will program your imagination for you is in the developing stages. In the meantime, continue with your imagination suppressants.

ADDENDUM FROM THE DEPARTMENT OF DEPTH

We realize that the public's impatience with life is due to their lack of success during this season's egg hunt and we take full responsibility for the hunt's failure. Many citizens have complained that the eggs were not only too cleverly hidden but were disguised as well and therefore we regret the confusion that the giant babies caused. The eggs, of course, were hidden in the babies' fists. But because the babies were hideous, deformed and mindless, as well as being giant, the public refused to approach them. We apologize for the distress and the deaths that subsequently occurred—the public wailing, the suicide epidemic. The giant babies, we believed, were a clever foil for the eggs, and we'd hoped that the public would be more enterprising in searching them out. We know that many citizens feel that something important has been left out of their lives and consequently devote much time and frenzy to the egg hunts in order to recover what they believe they have lost. It is regrettable that this season so few eggs were discovered; each egg contained a drop of wisdom in the form of a printed message imbedded in hexagonal prisms on the egg's surface. The failure of this season's egg hunt has meant that the public's imagination has been left in a dangerous state of flux.

In order to calm the widespread agitation, several of our staff will be on the road during the month of March. As a gesture of goodwill, the Department has initiated a replacement search, one which should not be too difficult for the public to grasp and which offers citizens an opportunity for levity.

Workers will be appearing incognito at public gatherings and the Department is pleased to issue two clues as to their identities:

Clue #1 – They will be alone, aloof, and bemused, indicating by their manner an overwhelming lack of need.

Clue #2 – During the course of conversation they will be imparting three new insights.

The job of each citizen is, first, to identify the field worker and then to engage him or her in conversation during which time the insights will be revealed in full. The three insights are about death, bagpipe music and balding men, and will be imparted in a lively and amusing manner. We are confident that these new insights will create in each citizen a feeling of joy.

A caution, however. The joy will be temporary, lasting only until the Department's next event, the annual giraffe sightings, when the public's mood will change to one of awe. Already several hundred giraffes are being groomed for the event, their long necks craning above their enclosures in anticipation of the sweet geranium plants which many citizens shyly place for them on their apartment balconies.

PAPER

That's right, Ma'am, we have only one piece of paper left and when we get another one we'll let you know. In the meantime you'll have to try working with empty spaces. There's much to be done with those. No, we don't know when to expect a second piece; these things aren't subject to any known predictions. Paper arrives when it will but we have our people working on it. The last paper storm was some years ago, on the Prairies, but because of the rush, much of it was ripped. And you know we can't predict the storms. As for free paper, it flutters from the heavens at odd occurrences, so there's no predicting that either. Why don't you try sitting under an oak tree at a full moon and see what happens? It could be some time before we get another piece in. Yes, we know it's difficult; our people suggest you try silence instead. Or if you're desperate, what about the margins of old books? Many have tried pasting margins together with some success although we agree it's not the same because of the flaking. Yes, we're sure you've used up your allotment of cardboard boxes but that's no reason to start crying. What about walls? Many are doing that now. The series of novel houses, each room a chapter. It's brought a revival of reader participation for those so inclined. Yes, we realize the electronic screen is useless, there's no taking it to bed and, no, you can't have this last piece of paper. Something of importance might have to be said. In the meantime, take a number and wait in line.

115

The practice of putting old people inside metal cages and placing them in schoolyards is to be discouraged. There is not one shred of evidence to support the view that this activity will retard the aging process. Our experiments with caged old people have shown that it is not possible to infuse youth; youth is not a scent that can be worn to dissolve the years. And hundreds of children swarming over such a cage, we have observed, will not result in the immediate suppleness of an old person's skin. If anything, under such conditions, old people become even more cranky than they already are; it has been reported that a number of children have been viciously scratched by the elderly trying to grab their arms and legs through the cage bars.

There are side-effects from the caging of old people, as well. Namely: they rapidly turn a dull yellow colour—both skin and clothing—which is unpleasant to view; they become adept at issuing profanities, delivered in the shriller tones of the musical scale; and if left unattended for longer than two weeks they turn into granite, an inferior type of stone of little use to the industrial world.

Our experiments further indicate that the youth of children cannot be extracted, rubbed off or otherwise worn with positive results by an old person. Practices such as jumping from schoolyard roofs into groups of children, smothering oneself with children at birthday parties, rolling with them under Christmas trees, or the wearing of small children on the back like a bulky shawl is of little use as is the practice of maintaining a child-like demeanour. For this reason, the Department of Experiments strongly suggests that old people abandon the pursuit of joy and return to their small, airless rooms. We find it distressing to witness their mindless capering on the public lawns—old men riding tricycles, old women dancing with each other in wedding dresses. The public lawns should be left to the solemn pursuit of childhood play.

URGENT MISSIVE CONCERNING THE BORING
WHITE WOMAN LOBBY

Even though it is the stated mandate of this Department to integrate minority groups into mainstream culture whenever and wherever possible, the Department is still not willing to entertain the demands from the Boring White Woman lobby. We are not yet convinced that they constitute a minority in the classic sense, despite their repeated attempts to convince us otherwise—the petitions, demonstrations, media events, and so forth. Events, we might add, which can only be described as exercises in pitiless whining. Furthermore, the Department rejects their claim that they constitute a minority group because they live—happily, they insist—with men. Attendance on children is also not proof of visible minority status and no amount of Mother's Day cards delivered to this office in black plastic bags will persuade us otherwise. Motherhood has been known to cross all boundaries, both of gender and colour, and is not the special domain of Boring White Women. In fact, we expect a public apology from the Boring White Woman lobby because of their challenge to our declaration that the old-style nuclear family is dead; we expect nothing less than their denouncing of this abhorrent fantasy.

The aim of this Department is the disbanding of the Boring White Woman lobby into more appropriate groupings—into one of the many victim groups, perhaps, or into associations for the specifically afflicted.

Staff are again reminded that fraternizing with Boring White Women will not be tolerated, and any Department member who attends a Boring White Woman event as a guest will be immediately dismissed. (Refer to the enclosed invitation, THE BORING WHITE WOMAN REVUE.) Such invitations are never harmless; Boring White Women are legendary for their guile and deviously feminine ways while maintaining an outer appearance of shallowness. In truth, they are extremists and their attempts to gain minority status are merely an infiltration tactic, a ploy to regain their formerly privileged position.

The influence of the Boring White Woman lobby must be countered at every turn; they've had enough special attention and their access to special programmes for minority groups will continue to be denied. Do not believe the Boring White Woman lobby when they claim they are lesbians, if not in body, then at least in heart.

Effective immediately, there will be a ban on Boring White Woman charity events. The Department of Diversity declares that citizens will no longer be won over by the obvious sentiment of such endeavours. The Diseases and the Poor will now be championed by one of the minority groups from our approved list, crushing once and for all, we believe, the irritatingly benevolent social worker image for which the Boring White Woman is renowned. As well, the following bans continue: bridge groups; committee work; self-help groups which focus on maintaining loving relationships with men; and mindless consumerism which, we now know, is the special province of Boring White Women.

Field workers are urged to continue in their derision of the Boring White Woman lobby, keeping in mind our recent and spectacular successes in dealing with their counterpart, The Dead White Male, now reduced to whimpering on the sidelines of history.

In closing, congratulations are due to those staff members who have successfully forayed into Boring White Woman territory—the suburbs. The Department is pleased to note that several of our favourite special interest groups are now operating within the public schools where they have wrested control of the parent-teacher agendas. It is cheering to see the Boring White Woman lobby marginalized to the status of hot dog server where it belongs. May they remain there.

DISASTERS

Field report: five households surveyed.

Household #1: All the disasters were pretty good but we liked the California earthquake the best because of the way the freeway bridge snapped in half like it was a pretzel. We liked seeing the survivors and rescuers tell their stories; they looked so beautiful on TV, so solemn and eloquent. Some even cried and we liked that; we appreciated the way the camera got up close to their faces, catching their tears in mid-flow.

Household #2: Watching the volcano erupt and the lava flow in its slow, deadly path towards the subdivision was pretty upsetting for everyone and we were glad there was a panel discussion after the show because our fears were erupting all over the living room and we needed reassurance. Volcano experts said eruptions only occur where there's a volcano, so we're glad we live on the flatlands; no lava's ever going to squish our house even though it looked nice in the TV picture, cracked grey and hot pink inside, quite lovely. What we have to worry about here is snakes and poisonous spiders and you should have a disaster show about them, the way the victims die and all that.

Household #3: We hated the hurricane; it was so boring. No rooftops flying, no cars flipping over. You do see a couple of black kids crouched beneath a freeway overpass and a lot of severely blown grass but so what? The only interesting thing was the way the hurricane dwarfed ordinary ranchers but we only got to see that for a couple of seconds. On the whole, don't bother with hurricanes again. Not unless we get to see some real destruction, squashed bodies and a lot of blood. We give the hurricane a 2.

Household #4: The flash flood in New Mexico made everyone mad. Because it served them right. There they were, a guy and a woman and her six-year-old daughter sitting on the roof of a pickup truck, stranded in the middle of a muddy, fast-flowing river. They shouldn't have been there in the first place, any idiot could see that. That guy was stupid (stupid!) to drive across the river. Several residents of the area even said as much. In future, if you're going to have a flash flood you'd better warn people not to drive through it. Watching that guy and woman and kid on top of the pickup for so long was really irritating. We could imagine the argument they were probably having because the guy figured he could make it and didn't. And not the kid's father, either, that was obvious—baseball cap, fat, and a beer drinker to boot, a low-life is what we figured. When the helicopter finally came our hearts went out to the Grandmother waiting on the shore with a blanket for the kid. Everyone here hopes she'll get custody of the kid because it's plain the mother has no sense when it comes to men; her choice nearly cost the kid her life.

Household #5: We think the Department should beef up its disaster series; this month's offerings were ordinary fare and we're getting bored with the show. The freak wave in Florida was a bust: an old woman toppled like a stick doll, a screaming ambulance, cars smashing against each other, a baby howling inside a semi-floating station wagon. Big deal. In our opinion, the Department needs to have death make an actual appearance. There needs to be bleeding bodies and hysterical, mourning mothers hurling themselves over the corpses. The closest the Department came to real-life disaster was during the earthquake: a car, a new Acura Integra, squashed under freeway overpass. The car was only eighteen inches high; a rescuing fireman said the car didn't have a chance. Now, that's a disaster!

Please add your suggestions to the preceding list keeping in mind that all disasters must be "natural"; i.e. not subject to political interference and not environmentally sensitive. Forthcoming disasters will focus on "killer" insects and reptiles, collapsing mountains—mudslides, avalanches, rock slides and the like—and freak windstorms, with an emphasis on toppling power lines and the spectacular profusion of life-threatening electrical sparks which can occur at these times.

SCAPE

WE ARE THE AMORPHOUS AUDIENCE NERVOUS FOR ANOTHER FUN FIX. WE DO NOT INTERACT, WE BEHOLD; WE VIEW, ARE TARGETED AS AUDIENCE, AS VIEWERS. WE ENGAGE AND DISENGAGE LIKE MOTORS. WE CLAP LIKE MORONS BEFORE SELECTED FUNNY MEN. THE FUNNY WOMEN ARE ALL UGLY. WE DISH IT UP; WE LIKE IT TASTELESS. WE COLOUR CO-ORDINATE OUR IDEAS TO MATCH THE PREVAILING WINDS, THIS YEAR NEON, NEXT YEAR RUST. THE ONLY RELIEF OCCURS WHEN FEAR BREAKS THROUGH THE FIFTEEN ALLOWABLE SHADES OF PLEASURE TO PANIC THE VIEWING HERDS OVER TV CLIFFS. WE'VE BECOME NO MORE THAN A CHIP OF AN HISTORICAL SOUND BYTE. NO MORE THAN EARLY BIRDS SHOPPING FOR THE ENDLESS BIRTH AND REBIRTH OF CELEBRITIES. THERE IS NO ESCAPING THE MARKET RESEARCHERS. WE ARE PIGEONS WITH A STARRING ROLE IN A VIDEO CALLED "TARGET PRACTICE." WE ARE BEING TAPED BEFORE A DEAD AUDIENCE. TOMORROW IS A POP SONG.

SECRETS

The terrorist group SPEIV (Society to Prevent the Eradication of Inner Voices) has resurfaced. Printed messages have been appearing randomly on citizens' home entertainment screens, on several of the giant television terminals which line the major free-ways, and on work screens at the Department of Silence. Public exposure has been limited because the duration of these messages has been brief and, to date, the public's distress level remains low. This, of course, could change in a matter of hours, erupting into the hysteria and gruesome public flagellations that occurred during previous SPEIV assaults. Officers should therefore be warned that a major SPEIV offensive may be in the offing. The following captured fragment may indicate the direction such an assault might take. It is reproduced and circulated under conditions of strict secrecy and will be the subject of the next departmental meeting. Department members may wish to take a reaction suppressant before reading it.

... *the Department of Secrets says* THERE ARE NO SECRETS. *But we say there are many secrets. Here are some of them:*

1. The idea of the unknown has been obliterated; what's palpable has been made unknowable enough.

2. Your consciousness has been willingly limited; any "other" reality is now classified as mental illness.

3. Your consciousness has fled; your consciousness is in hiding.

4. The subversive wing of SPEIV *operates under the name "The Rules & Regulations of an Institute called Tranquillity" in celebration of our spiritual mentor, William Hone (circa 1807), the great English satirist who pioneered the role of the public informer. Who throughout his works said, "conscience makes cowards of us all." Who dared to ridicule royalty, self-serving governments and all oppressors of vibrant, questioning thought. We are proud to call ourselves Honers, to sharpen our wit, to perform our random assaults in his honour. To gather together voicing our rallying cry:* EVERYTHING MUST BE QUESTIONED. *We dedicate ourselves to splendour and diversity. We are the protectors of the unforeseen, the perpetuators and guardians of the novel. Join us. Imagine a strange singing, a mechanical choir erupting from the cities like the whistles and clanking of broken pipes. It is still possible for our silenced voices to be heard ...*

WORD OF MOUTH
1996

REFUSAL

SLAP

First there was a slap. Two slaps, one on either cheek. *Don't interrupt me when I'm on the phone!* Slaps you'd see a princess give a nobody in a movie, or a maid, or a workman. Smack, smack. Like that. Quick. With the hand that fed, that washed the body, that brushed the hair. Slaps like the sound of sudden gunfire, unpredictable. And the war zone: the living room, the narrow hallway where the telephone rang.

She must have placed the phone under her chin, must have positioned it carefully so she could slap with ease. *Come here while I slap you.* No, it was the pulling at her skirt, at the long slim high-heeled legs that did it. Close enough for her to whirl around, one hand free. And a dummy child in place to receive it, not figuring it out in time, always too close, always surprised and shocked. A sudden slap like the slap of birth, or of insight.

ANGELS

There's a house at the foot of a steep hill, a rented house with dusty passageways and hidden rooms, with balconies overlooking a large wood-panelled living room, a castle of a house. In an upstairs bedroom there are angels. Yes, angels, you're sure of it. Three in white gowns, two in blue, with thick, waxy wings. Hovering at the end of your bed; one is floating near the ceiling, its golden hair brushing the overhead light. Angels living—if that's what angels do—in your room. They don't speak but their presence is so claustrophobic you scream. Scream and scream. Their presence is sucking the air from the room, but they're smiling at you warmly, like Bible drawings of Jesus, and their smiles never change. Smiling while they eat your air.

Quit imagining things, you're later told. *Come down to earth.*

HANDLESS

This woman who slaps. What of her? Oh, you keep away from her, at least you try, keep her at arm's length, refused. Because a nightmare is having your arms cut off below the elbows. There's so much blood when you push her away. But still she grabs, still she slaps.

Why won't you call her Mother? Because the word sticks hard in your throat like a growl and won't form into music?

Instead, you call her the slapping woman.

BROWN

What does the slapping woman look like? Is she beautiful? Is she a beautiful, wicked Queen? No, not beautiful though she has a certain grace, like the cold stiffness of a China figurine.

But everything about her is brown. Like dirt? Yes, like dirt. From her thin hair to her dull-brown eyes, from her tailored suits and her alligator high-heeled shoes to the fox-fur she wears when going out, draped around her shoulders like a live thing. Two tiny fox heads with yellow glass eyes staring at you from either side of her neck.

MUD PIES

In the back yard you mould the slapping woman out of mud and twigs, a whole family of mud-pie women, some larger and more fierce than the others, some small and helpless. When the mud is powdery dry, you have wars with them, smashing them together until they crumble, until armies of perishing slapping women are strewn in broken clumps about the ground.

You use twigs for their arms and legs because her bones are so sharp they hurt you when you're held. Twigs that snap easily in half, then snap in half again.

LAPS

Tea in the living room. She pulls you onto her lap in front of a neighbour woman. Her knees are sharp through her brown skirt; it's difficult to balance, to sit still without falling off.

She's being careful with you, formal, slow. No, you couldn't call it kindness, but her voice is even, a silky veil, a kind of song. She's talking to the woman about her home, far away, across the ocean. *The sun shines all the time in Australia. Just shines and shines. Not like here where there's nothing but rain.*

Warily you let her hold you, soothed by the delicious sound of her newly soft voice.

Her slapping hands for the moment lying still.

MUSIC

A crowd of strangers with drinks in their hands have gathered around the piano at the far end of the living room. The slapping woman is playing "Kitten on the Keys," "The Twelfth Street Rag," "Hernando's Hide-Away." Everyone is singing. You're sitting on the piano bench beside her plunking at the high end of the keyboard, at those shrill notes that are never used. Miraculously you're at the heart of things, ignored.

Once during these times she calls you *Darling* and strokes your hair. Darling!

Play us another one! Something we can get our teeth into. Play "Too-Ra-Loo-Ra-Loo-Ra." Play "My Heart Is Like A Red, Red Rose."

Darling! The music of that rare caress.

THE FATHER

She's given him your plate with the cut-up meat. Then laughs and laughs. Standing at his side, she's feeding him the meat, one piece at a time. *Be a good boy and eat your supper!* And he's laughing too, his head's thrown back, his wide mouth open. Oh, the bells of that private laughter! His paper napkin at his throat like a bib. He's holding his mouth like a hungry bird, she's teasing him with the meat. *Don't be a naughty boy!* Making him bend after it, further and further, until he falls off the chair.

PRISON

The slapping woman is shouting. Throwing plates of food against the kitchen cupboards, a bowl of stewed prunes, a gravy boat against the kitchen door after the father's retreating back. A white door, brown gravy.

Once again she's crying. *I want to go home. I hate this country, and all this rain. It's a prison. I hate everything about it.*

D ressed in a night-gown, you're running circles around the edge of
the living room rug, jumping on the armchairs, keeping time to
"The Teddy Bear's Picnic." Play the record again! And again! The
Father's on the floor beneath a lamp holding a needle and pink thread,
sewing doll's underpants. And a cape! And a doll's skirt made from a
piece of cut-up pillowcase. Threading elastic with a safety pin through
a crude waistband. *I learned how to sew at sea, on the ships at night. We
had to do our own mending.*

You're sitting on the living room rug with the Father eating toast
and jam. Then the floor's a heaving black ocean with orange circle
islands made from the light of table lamps and you're a sailor hopping
from one circle to the next. *Yo ho ho.* The Father's clapping his hands.
And a bottle of rum.

GONE

Where is the slapping woman?

She's gone.

Gone like a drifting fog because her departure is so quiet. She's slipped out at night, floated through the bedroom ceiling with the angels.

You've looked up from your playing, turned around at the supper table and she's not there. You weren't watching and she stole away. You weren't watching and she's slapped you again.

BOAT

Why won't you eat? The Father's given you all your favourite foods: chocolate cake and ice cream, fish and chips, orange pop, jelly beans, marshmallows. You should be happy; this should be a celebration, she's gone away. Why won't you speak? *Cat got your tongue?*

But there are no words for this emptiness, it's too large to name. You long for her slippery legs, for the hands that once stroked your hair. Without her presence you feel eerily alone.

The Father rocks you on his lap. He reads to you: *Winnie-the-Pooh, The Owl and the Pussycat.* You cry and cry, adrift in your sadness. You're clinging to a ball that's too wide for your grasp. Hold onto the Father, he's a sailor, he won't let you drown. Listen he's telling you a story: *She's gone away on a boat, maybe never to return.*

She's sailed in a boat, in a pea-green boat, she's slapping the ocean blue.

BOOK

In the living room of the castle house. You're helping the Father put toys into a large cardboard box.

And where will I love?

You mean live?

Yes, where will I live?

With your Grandma on the Island. And I'll visit every weekend. You can make me toast and jam, and we'll take rides in the car and go to the beach.

And stand on the shore, and wave at the waves, and stare at the boats in the distance.

And what about your tricycle? Do you want to take that?

Oh yes. And the doll and the doll's clothes and all the books. Hans Christian Andersen. *The Princess and the Pea. The Snow Queen.* The Snow Queen! *There once was a child who lived frozen inside …*

Pushing aside the toys you take hold of the Father's hand.

WHAT'S TRUE, DARLING
1997

Dorothy Parker's Dog

When I came home from the hospital I discovered my friends had redecorated my room at the Algonquin. They'd draped the bed and writing desk, the couch and chairs in black cloth and they'd hung things from the ceiling—framed pictures of condemned murderers, carving knives dangling from strings. There was even a length of rope draped artfully across my bed. And they'd placed an assortment of step ladders around the desk in case I felt like climbing. The effect was bleak but charming. Ironic decor.

They thought I'd be pleased. I was pleased, after a fashion. By the gesture of the thing. Who were these friends? I don't know, the usual blur of revved-up people. Somebody this, somebody that. What does it matter who they were? Background music, bit players, atmosphere for the macabre piece.

But whoever they were they got the idea from me, from what I'd done while in hospital. You see, I'd attached a small orchid corsage to each of my bandaged wrists. Yes I did, nasty of me, I know, but it made me laugh at the time, gave me a kind of grim satisfaction. Perhaps I'd ordered the corsages from a florist myself, perhaps I'd sent one of my friends to fetch them. I don't remember. But the orchids were pale mauve in colour and hard as wax. And I had this delicious thought: I will be a sarcophagus, flowers sprouting from my near-bloodless form. Cleopatra. That's who I had in mind. I'll be Cleopatra lying in my hospital bed, pale and calm, my corsaged wrists lying still above the covers.

I received my friends like this, visiting hours being the same time as cocktail hours, four to six. When they saw me they screamed with laughter. *Oh, our Dotty's so wicked!* And opened the champagne bottles and the bottles of Scotch. We drank to my cleverness. Thirty or forty friends partying in my hospital room. All the twinkling New York gnats were there—writers, editors, the round table drunks, all the bright young things. I got fairly lit mixing the Scotch with the sleeping tablets; after that I was gone for days.

How many times did I attempt suicide? Every time a party ended. Every time I put pen to paper.

Doesn't that sound grand? But it's a full-fledged lie. Which, of course, I excelled at. Lies and more lies. Here she lies and I don't mean Cleopatra. Oh the wordy girl! Suicide or murder; I was adept at both though it was by pure accident, this trickery with words.

For some reason I was called upon by the New York circle to train as their magician. And the first thing I learned was running with my nose to the ground. Oh, I could sniff out the idiots! *You can lead a whore to culture but you can't make her think.* You see, I was a natural; spite and sarcasm flowed easily. This is where my fame lay—in the caustic line, harsh enough to wither any reputation! People were delighted, craved the personal insult. The more they laughed, the nastier I got until a party wasn't a party until I was there.

But there were things I loved more than words: Scotch and dogs top the list. I've always preferred a dog to a man and I've had a string of both. I can remember all of my dogs' names—but the names of the men! Not one.

Robinson was my favourite dog, a Dachshund; he went everywhere with me. Our day began at five with cocktails in my room at the Algonquin. Now you're not to believe the reports that Robinson shit on the rug. People assumed this because I never rose before noon and where would the poor dog do his business? Where indeed? On the pages of the *New York Times*, where else? Spread about the floor, awaiting Robinson's anointment. Since waking up was not the best part of my day, jittery and bitchy as I often was, inspecting Robinson's deposits gave me a small pleasure, like a throw of the dice: Robinson the fortune teller; I was always delighted to see whose writing he'd chosen to shit upon—some upstart critic venturing onto my turf, some pathetic reviewer attempting a Parker line (everyone knew I was Constant Reader at the *New Yorker*).

So Robinson was my researcher. And the smell? There was no smell. Darling, that's the beauty of hotel life: maids. Each day at four they'd come in to clean, air the place out. And then at five cocktails began. Twenty or thirty people would stream in bearing gifts—I loved receiving gifts—usually bottles of Scotch or little things to eat or a toy for Robinson. Everyone drinking and laughing, everyone so gay, and then all of us piling into taxis for a night at the clubs, Robinson tucked beneath my arm like an enormous sausage.

At the clubs he'd curl himself beneath the table. A group of us drinking and there Robinson would be fast asleep. (Something I'd always wished men would do: sleep at my feet.) But he'd start awake and follow me whenever I moved; he'd even follow me to the Ladies and wait outside the stall. Such devotion! I'd order waiters to bring him bowls of water or chopped meat, and many of the young men hanging about would be called upon to take him outside to do his business in the street. And they daren't refuse me. After all, I had them by the short hairs: Refusal to do their duty by Robinson meant banishment from my terrible, envied circle. And not one of them would risk that!

A wonderful dog, Robinson. Cecil Beaton begged for months to take my picture and I only consented if Robinson could be in the picture as well. I told Cecil: You mustn't photograph me close-up, I detest that sort of inspection—you must take my picture from a distance, as if I'm glimpsed from across a room at a crowded party or a hotel lobby, as if people were saying, "Ah, there goes Mrs. Parker. You know who Mrs. Parker is, don't you? Why, she's … " The darling of the New York art world, I might have added—the *enfant terrible* at the heart of the literary scene.

The picture Cecil finally settled on as his creation has me seated formally, a side shot facing left. I'm dressed for the outdoors in a hat, a long coat with a fur collar and holding a fur muff; you only see half of my face which was fine with me—I've never been terribly excited by my own face, too tiny and dark for my liking. In this picture Robinson is placed on the ground and facing me so that his body is in profile as well; his head is cocked, his muscular body taut, expectant.

My beloved Robinson; I never let him out of my sight. He even escorted me when I spoke to the Dream Come True Club. This was during the height of my fame—people couldn't get enough of me. It was a very swank club in the upper Eighties; several hundred members turned out. After a fine meal of Scotch and more Scotch I rose from my perch at the head table and gave the speech.

I told the audience how I'd really wanted to be a famous fire-eater, wearing a black sequined gown and a red feathered hat, the flame in my torch threatening to immolate me there and then. I told them that this writing of words is pale by comparison—there's no hooplah, no costumes, no real danger. Any fire we writers consume is of our own making—the stuff of sound and air—and if our words are not hot enough, do not set hearts and minds aflame, if what we hurl into the world doesn't catch fire ...

The applause was generous, the audience pleased. They liked how I had settled for second best, this writing of stories and verse. Afterwards several of them asked for my recipe for writing success and I wrote it down on small index cards: three parts bullshit, one part spit.

Shortly after, I told this story at a party of Edna's. Oh I was lit. The party was to celebrate something or other; we were never short of things to celebrate. Edna's new book of poems perhaps. We were all gathered in the garden because Edna was showing us her outdoor writing table, a perfectly boring wood table set beneath the trees. Who the hell cares about her writing table? I mentioned as much to a man standing beside me. Darling, I told him, you wouldn't believe where I write my things—in bed, on the john, in the back seats of taxis. Oh, I do believe I'll conduct a tour of my john the next chance I get, I told him, and he laughed.

Anyway people went on and on about Edna's table, several of the crowd slobbering, practically licking the cursed thing when this odious woman, one of those overly dressed society matrons, bosom extending from neck to knee, spoke up, declaring to Edna: So this is where you do it! This is where you construct your famous poems. Reaching up to the overhead sky with those skilful hands and grabbing fistfuls of dappled light. Stirring this light into your poems. So that's how it's done; this is why your poems glow.

You want glow, I shouted, I'll bet you've never seen a fire-eater. And I flicked my lighter, arched my neck and opened my mouth. The crowd gasped, jumped back, then fled. Edna grabbing her book of poems lest they fall prey to a stray spark. Everyone gathering inside the house to sip champagne and pop cool cucumber sandwiches into their admiring mouths. (My mouth has never admired anything.)

Leaving me to perform alone in the garden with Robinson as my only audience. It was a wonderful performance. Not a flame wasted, not a delicate nose hair singed. A performance executed smoothly and in the grand eccentric tradition. I am, after all, an *idiot savant* for beauty.

There we were in the garden. My grandest performance. With Robinson watching, panting and blinking his applause.

Closing Time at Barbie's Boutique

"The problem," Barbie said to Skipper, "is the ones with fat arms and purple-white skin. They buy something sleeveless and want to wear it home. Then you have to reach up to their fetid armpits and cut the tag. It can knock you over."

"I hate the ones without underpants," said Skipper. "Yesterday a woman trying on a jump-suit wanted help with the buttons and right there in front of me was her bush. No way was I going near that thing."

"What did you do?" asked Barbie.

"Nothing," said Skipper. "They all think you're their mother: love them, love their bush, don't care how they look. I just hung the jump-suit back on the rack and hoped some dummy doesn't get a social disease from trying it on. I'm just thankful I don't have pubic hair."

"Amen to that," said Barbie.

"I wish," though, said Skipper, "that I didn't feel so miserable. Sometimes being human seems almost attractive."

"Bite your perfect lips," said Barbie. "What you need is a change. Why don't you do something with those braids?"

"Yes, I could definitely do with a change," said Skipper.

"You should get out more," said Barbie. "Have a few laughs. Too bad I'm saving seal pups in the Arctic next weekend."

"Couldn't I come along?"

"Not this time," said Barbie. "I promised Ken. He's taking pictures of me for my Christmas Sticker Book."

"Oh," said Skipper. "Tough tit, them's the breaks."

"Cheer up," said Barbie. "Think about the seventeen midgets in here last week wanting car coats."

"That was funny," said Skipper. "Or the time the hunchback wanted an evening gown."

"Yes, that was a laugh," said Barbie. "Very funny. Then there was that bus load of women all celebrating their one-hundredth birthdays. Came in just to look around. Erotic pawing of lingerie."

"I liked the male nurses," said Skipper.

"They all slobbered," said Barbie. "I saw them slobbering. Drooling, lusting beasts."

"I could do with one of those," said Skipper. "A drooling, lusting beast would just about fit the bill."

"Never heard from Brad again? Where'd he get to?"

"A younger model," said Skipper. "Traded me in for a younger model. One of those new flexible jobs that bends at the knees. A stick with legs. Why do these things happen? What's the matter with perpetual twelve?"

"Nothing's the matter with perpetual twelve," said Barbie. "At least you're not close to mature. Like that antique in here this morning. Did you see her fingernails? Enough dirt in there to start a rooftop herb garden. Wanted polyester."

"Figures," said Skipper.

"Even so," said Barbie, "I have my principles. I won't sell something that looks bad on a customer."

"Unless," said Skipper.

"Unless," said Barbie, "they're beyond hope. And many are beyond hope. Most are beyond hope."

"The flowered silk on the fatties," said Skipper.

"The black and purple bikinis on the stringy broads looking like they're on their last bag of dog food," said Barbie.

"How do you do it?" said Skipper. "How do you keep Ken?"

"Well," said Barbie, "I'm always light and gay and full of fun. Plus I'm not bad looking."

"You're a knockout," said Skipper. "You're a beautiful American doll."

"Make the most with what you've got," said Barbie. "Work on your personality."

"If only I had your hair, your perfect nipple-less breasts," said Skipper.

"Well you *are* supposed to be only twelve," said Barbie.

"I want your longer legs," said Skipper. "Your Crystal Barbie Gown."

"Always look on the bright side," said Barbie. "Learn to be a good sport. In a pinch, dreamboats like Ken just love plucky little girls who are good sports."

"I'll bet," said Skipper. "Like the one in here on Tuesday? Ooze of good sport?"

"Not that much good sport," said Barbie. "Horse teeth, saddle thighs. It makes you wonder. People, they're quite revolting. The one in here on Groundhog Day. A walking cadaver."

"Sequined suit, no bum?"

"The very one," said Barbie. "Imagine being all tarted up at eighty! Bird bones dressed as nouvelle cuisine. Imagine having a life and having it just about over."

"It boggles the acrylic hair," said Skipper.

"Thank Mattel we're spared all that," said Barbie. "The worst that can happen to us is competition from newer, more supple models. But they'll never have the prestige we have. We were here first; we're quality."

"You really think so?" said Skipper.

"Of course," said Barbie. "We're number one. We've been around a long time and we're still as firm as ever. You've still got your original lip paint! And consider this: we lose a leg, no problem, a new one can always be found—whole businesses are devoted to manufacturing parts for us. And you can't say that about the human models; it's the green garbage bags for them before long."

"The worst that can happen to us," said Barbie, "is being left too long in the sun—the slow melt of our features. Or being tossed from a car window by an unpleasant child. Or being left to soak too long in the bathtub and having black mould growing around our neck, arm, and leg holes. And even if some child cuts off all our hair, it can be replaced in any colour we want. But it's best not to dwell on negative things. That's Barbie's Motto. And when you think of it, most of us are cherished and you can't say that about humans. And we have the best, most fashionable wardrobes, too. Some of us even have our own Boutiques! And swimming pools! And Southern Mansions!"

"I fear the feminists," said Skipper. "The leather pants and crew cut brigade. They'd be happy if we didn't exist. They'd like nothing better than to melt us down for dildos."

"Nonsense," said Barbie, "They probably played with us when they were little. Everyone's had a Barbie."

"I don't like the sound of that," said Skipper.

"Are you still fretting about Brad?" said Barbie. "Look on the bright side. At least you don't have a hairless head. Like the one in here on Hallowe'en."

"What did it want?" said Skipper. "Trick or treat?"

"Combat boots," said Barbie.

"Ha, ha," said Skipper. "I think I'm feeling better."

"Good," said Barbie. "If you stay close to your sister Barbie, you'll concentrate on the carefree days of youth, your days will be filled with adventures and you'll always be smiling. Now don't you think it's better to be a doll?"

"Yes. Yes I do," said Skipper.

"I'm glad to hear it," said Barbie. "Now help me unpack this carton. It has my new Swiss Chalet inside and I can't wait to try on my new ski fashions. And if you promise to keep smiling and keep that pretty little head of yours empty, I just might find something in here for you to try on, too."

JIGSAW

Oh that Leonard Cohen. He turns up when you'd least expect him. Dinner time, for example, when we're sitting down to our meagrer meal, our Gregorian Chant meal, it being several lifetimes before payday. I was just dishing up the beans to those of us humbly assembled and turned to my left and there he was sitting next to Henny calm as you please.

I'm very fond of beans, Leonard Cohen said, looking searchingly into my eyes, lingering he was in my eyes, we were having what you might call a moment of hesitation across a sea of beans. And I said, yes, I love beans too, they being high on my list, right up there at the top of my list of poverty food, and I love a man who loves beans. And Henny, a man who's loved without hesitation, said yes, good old beans, we all enjoy a satisfying meal of beans, but not any beans, not canned beans or boiled beans or fried or sautéed beans but *raw beans*, these being the most economical way to consume bean nutrition and we're everything for nutrition at this table, yes everything, because sometimes there's little else to think of.

Leonard Cohen smiled, I believe it was wisely, and slowly nodded his head, his dark-haired head with its sculpted Roman nose and its cheeks flushed a scandalous hint of pink. I was about to ask him his thoughts on the culture of beans, his views on this subject, but first I said, surely there's poetry in beans. And he smiled again into my brown beanie eyes and said, yes, dear lady, there's poetry in beans, in figs, in cashew nuts, you name it, we're rolling in poetry, it's just a matter of being Aldous Huxley and opening the doors, peeling the eyeballs, baring the skin and this is often everything. In fact, he continued, I'm sure there's more skin in the world than asphalt and if all the skin was laid flat, laid end to end, we'd have a new membrane with which to cover the earth, replacing ozone, replacing our dank and fumey skies. Yes, I said, baring our skin is a necessary concept because that's what the children are doing this very minute, razor blading their emotions with the help of Aldous Huxley and blotter acid. Can't you hear them howling? I asked, a cluster of children at the back of the house howling their heads off that the sky is falling, the sky is falling, not liking their eyeballs flayed, not liking it at all?

Leonard waved his hand. It means nothing, he said, nothing at all. But I was impelled by the urgent something and had to leave Leonard Cohen to eat his beans alone as we, the rest of us at the table, but principally Henny and me, rushed to quell the children's hysteria. Hysteria of the usual kind, to be sure, but raw hysteria, that being the best way to consume new emotion, new vision, which is what the children were doing. By the time I'd handed out the blankets, re-read the old stories and settled the children, I found Leonard sitting outside on a collapsible deck chair jotting in a notebook, serene Buddha that he most certainly is. (But a wee bit disinclined for all that, I thought, to get his pinkies wet, his elbows muddied.)

Henny then said, as we rested in the sun at Leonard's feet, Henny said, well Leonard Cohen, since we're all liberals here, can you tell me your views on nothingness? But didn't get to expand on his theme because Leonard got mad, got huffy and said, I never defend a thing I've researched. And with this utterance got up and strode out of the yard.

So there's another piece of the puzzle gone missing and if this keeps up we won't have a puzzle at all, just a series of holes and spaces. You start out life with the puzzle intact like an enormous jigsaw and then one by one the pieces drop out or go missing; every time you ask a question, shake your head and admit you just don't know, a piece of the puzzle goes missing. Every time you approach a Leonard or a Don or a Julio or a Grace and ask them to tell you why and how, it's tits up for another piece. If all the holes and missing spaces were laid end to end, I said to Henny, if all the unanswered questions were gathered into a giant bouquet … And Henny sighed, gazing about the empty yard. Nobody here but us chickens, he said. And we left it at that, returning to the supper table and our meal of beans. Nodding our heads. Pecking at our plates of beans.

HALLOWE'EN SO FAR AWAY

Home and the undressing begins. Suits, dresses, overalls, masks. The workday world becoming a pile of clothing and props heaped at the living room door. It's evening now and we can relax, sip cocktails, become who we really are.

Some of us are seven feet tall! And the day has been a torture of smallness, folded as we are into three-piece suits. Our bodies cramped, our limbs bonsai'd into awkward shapes. What a relief to finally stretch; two full strides and we're in the kitchen pouring wine.

The hunchback's relieved, as well. He's spent the day as a cashier at Volume Discount wearing a harness so he'll look like everyone else. But his hump is aching, his back sore from standing straight. Now he removes the binding that conceals his form, and the glass eye that hides his empty socket. Removes the platform shoe from his left leg allowing his game leg to drag free.

There are others, too. A witch removes her teeth and blonde wig, settling onto the sofa, gin and tonic in hand. What a pleasure to leave the library behind, allow her voice its wondrous range; cackling and shrieking she pulls bent fingers through dry, black hair. And executive secretaries, ward room nurses: from their backs unfold fairy wings as delicate as origami sculptures; now they can draw their curtains, hover about the light fixtures without gossip or scorn.

Home, and even used-car salesmen are transformed, rushing to bathroom sinks and erasing workday faces to find relief: vampire pallor and bloody lips exposed. And teachers! Peeling off their teacher masks a clown face erupts; sore red noses are massaged into bulbous shapes, enormous feet spring forth from Cinderella shoes. But some of us *are* Cinderella, we cry, hiding our prettiness inside stiff power suits. Our days spent as businesswomen, entrepreneurs; we've been talking out the sides of our mouths, shouting down the opposition. Now we can don our rags, wash our floors in peace. Dreaming of rescue—the Hallowe'en Ball. Only in the sanctity of our homes, this revealing; our one public night so far away.

Only at home. Where the Kings and Queens amongst us can tear off drab workday clothes. We've spent the day disguised as bureaucrats faking humility. Now we can unleash our secret majesty, anoint one another with the tissue-covered crowns we hide in our dresser drawers. We're lighting the candles, filling the goblets, discussing over dinner our plans for the realm. How much to spend on the dependents? The children, the dog, the cleaning lady who acts like a serf? How much for the banquet, the RRSPs, the winter vacation, the ermine robe? And which bloody daytime war will next receive our royal assent?

Blague Mountain

In desperation, then, some of us disfigured ourselves in the name of Art. Becoming the Slasher Poets, razor-blading haikus onto our backs and thighs. Others of our kind found success as Tattooed Children's Writers, covering our bodies with illustrations from our books—a special privilege for children now, the live performance, curious hands tracing the figures displayed on our colourful backs and arms. Some women poets shaved their heads—not the whole head just the top—in a simulation of male-pattern baldness and then combed thin strands over their shiny domes. And founded a School, a Movement, calling it Blague Mountain—a raucous gathering of semi-bald, drunken, flannel-shirt wearing, cigar smoking, women poets whose Anti-Minimalist Manifesto included celebrating the adjective, the formerly reviled and dependent adjective—and some writers were allowed to join the movement and some were not. Other writers turned to history, plundering the look of another time and so costuming became important—ball gowns, uplift bras; there was a flurry of romance writers exposing their breasts on national TV. Amongst male fiction writers, cardinal's robes appeared at book launches. And nun's habits, Gilbert & Sullivan pirates, three-piece suits from the jugular of the corporate world. All for media interest. All for the coveted author profile, the scant review. The work is supposed to speak for itself, one novelist complained, but it takes too long to say what it has to say. This from the woman who had a hair implant on her chin and upper lip thus becoming The Bearded Lady Novelist, renowned on three continents …

THE PARTY

The party's over but I don't want it to end. I've barricaded the door with the couch and hat stand, spreadeagled my body against the hallway entrance. Desperate, desperate because it's too early for the guests to leave. Their coats are hidden. I called a cab. Their coats are piled on the back seat of a cab bound for Duncan B.C. Deliver the coats to the Chamber of Commerce, I told the driver, or give the coats to the needy. I told him: If you can't find any needy in Duncan B.C. or if the needy in Duncan B.C. don't want the coats, then take them to Nanaimo or Port Alberni. If necessary take the ferry to Vancouver; it's my treat, no expense is too great to keep the guests at the party. Yes, clothe the needy. The streets of Vancouver are awash with people going coatless and hatless. It's winter and everyone's needing a decent coat. There's a navy-blue topcoat in a cashmere blend. Several Gortex jackets, wonderful for keeping the rain off shivering bodies. And my guests won't be needing their coats. Not when they'll be staying at my party having the time of their lives. Saying things like: This is the best party; how do you do it? We're so grateful you invited us; it must be a charming life to have such charming parties; and the food and music, you certainly know how to make a splash. There are many fine coats and hats amongst my guests' effects. Did I mention the fake fur cape? The selection of Eddie Bauer toques? The watchcaps? The red felt fedora? Such fine heads for these fine hats to sit upon! With smart haircuts and every one of them blown dry. But they mustn't leave. Not yet. Don't let the guests leave! My mission in life. I've suddenly found it! Keep the guests at the party at all costs! None of this brooding, solitary nonsense. None of these couples with their cold and cranky conversations driving off into the dull night. No, what my guests need is converting to the festive cause. They don't think I've noticed the eye contact over the canapés, the slight nodding of heads between couples, the pause in the party talk, the chatter, the birdsong in the kitchen going suddenly mute, the whispers between themselves, the ill-concealed yawns. Meaning: Time to head out, thanks so much for the party but we really have to go, I'm not feeling well, she's not feeling well, nobody here is well, but your party was delightful, the food so thoughtfully placed about the room, the peanuts, the veggie platter, and the music just so, what was that arresting music anyway, acid jazz? Never heard it before, an acquired taste, we're sure, like oysters or olives, but so interesting and we must get together soon. Grabbing purses, delivering wine glasses to the sideboard. So polite! But there's this groundswell of guests gathering themselves to leave. When the first ones make for the door there's no stopping the flood of guests swarming off my stage. But I won't allow it, will I? I'll stop them in their tracks. I won't allow this false joviality, these preparations to leave. Leaving. Leaving my party. I threw a party. Everyone came, then left too soon. It's barely dark out. This is an outrage. An insult. Why did they even come in the first place if they planned to leave so soon? But won't they be shocked when they can't find their coats? When they find the windows boarded up. There's my husband Martin on the ladder with a sheet of plywood, hammering window after window. Well done, darling, soon enough we'll be turning up the music, dishing out the chili. There's hours and hours of fun left yet. What's the matter with you people? Forgotten how to have fun? What does it take? More booze? More dope? A three-piece band positioned by the fireplace? Was the guest list not to your liking? Listen, when I have a party I expect you to stay a week, have a bath, sleep on the living room floor. I expect you to dance and dance your silly feet off. Turn up the music, Martin, let the guests have the time of their lives. Why else have a party? Think of history. In medieval times guests were better trained. A party lasted days. Even the Catholic Church had parties. Unbelievable as it is, once the church had 197 official feast days. Now if that isn't a party organ what is? Even in the last century our very own Canadian farmers in the prairie heartland bundled children and dogs into the wagons heading for a central farm, staying a week, sometimes two, getting drunk and dancing to that old-timey fiddle music. You must have seen the movies of simple farmer folk kicking up their heels. Like that. Or think of Hemingway's Spain, *The Sun Also Rises.* Think of carnivals in South America. You can't have a carnival over a polite sip of wine and one or two crackers, then a rush out the door. A carnival takes longer than an hour and a half—it takes a lifetime. Even our own idle rich during the early part of this century went in for long parties, several days at least, covering every shade and nuance of party life. They had cocktails before dinner and dressed up— tuxedos and taffeta, earrings and pearls. Then they played cards and danced to the gramophone, drank port, went for strolls in the garden. They changed their clothes several times a day. Went off to their guest beds and not always with their own partner. Next day it was a full breakfast and horse riding or tennis or swimming then lunch then a nap then more cocktails and another outfit and another dinner. And it went on like this for days. We've copied everything else from the early rich but why haven't we copied their parties? I'll tell you why— it's because we're constipated. Our celebrations are squeezed out; they're dry hard things. And they're that way because you don't know how to be a guest. You thought you'd arrive late and leave early. You thought you'd make an appearance then slip away unnoticed. You thought you'd leave my party too soon. Well, we've sent off your coats, we've boarded up the doors and windows—you won't get away so easily. Even if we have to tie you up, make you listen to a selection of our music, even if we have to imprison you, goddamnit, you're going to have a good time. You're going to kick off your shoes and dance on the living room rug; you're going to have talks in the wee hours, philosophical talks that will deepen your lives. But I can see you don't agree. You're objecting to the gun, to my husband's use of force, you don't like being herded back into the living room, made to sit on the couches and kitchen chairs. One of you has shouted *terrorists.* One of

159

you has screamed *hostage* trying to crawl off and dial 911. All of you wanting rescue. Imagine! Wanting rescue from this celebration of life! Do as you're told and nobody will get hurt. You know how these things go; you've watched enough hostage dramas on TV. Just stay calm, keep your heads down, don't make eye contact with each other, don't upset the one with the gun. Martin, my poor darling, he's doing all this for me. He didn't even want a party. What, Loralee, he said, another party? But I convinced him. Look I said, we'll give it one last try—maybe it's been the menu, maybe the lighting. He didn't expect things to get out of hand but he was prepared—the plywood, the nails, and now the nylon rope and the gun. Well, what did you expect? Don't you understand we're saving you from your own joyless lives? Think of this as a deprogramming session. A few days with us and you'll definitely know what the festive experience is all about. And really, all I required was that you stay longer at my party. Like the song—"Stay Just A Little Bit Longer." Your babysitters wouldn't have minded, what's an extra hour? They'd be grateful for the pay. And what harm would there have been, what's an hour or two of lost sleep if the evening was worth it? But, oh no, you couldn't stick it. You had to make your excuses. Midnight! I would have been content with midnight! But it's only nine-fifteen. Never mind, there's plenty of time now. Days and days. So let's get started. On the count of three, I want everyone laughing. I want mirth on your faces. You can still laugh with your hands and feet bound. With your mouths taped shut. That shouldn't trouble you. So start laughing. That's good. The animated nodding of heads. Also good. I appreciate your getting into the spirit of things. Louder. Now keep that up. I'm just going into the kitchen. Martin will watch you. I'm going to sit alone at the kitchen table listening to your joyful laughing. A pause before the party games begin. Sipping my wine in contentment. Listening to the fabulous party going on behind the kitchen door.

ALL CHICKENS ARE SUCKS:
NOTES FROM THE LITSHOW

1. A man asks if he can pray before I begin a reading, kneeling in the cafe and asking for God's protection. This was in a dream. The same dream in which my reading was sabotaged by a young Jehovah's Witness poet who flung my books into a bank of blackberry vines.

2. I give a reading on a B.C. ferry. Over a hundred Japanese tourists are in attendance. All of them are asleep except for one who is manning a video camera. It occurs to me that I often see Japanese tourists sleeping en route—heads slumped against bus windows, bodies leaning into each other in airport lounges. But there are always one or two taking pictures. Perhaps they draw straws to pick who will stay awake and do the filming. Perhaps they gather, later on at home, on their day off from the corporation, to view these slides and videos. All of them amazed and delighted by what they slept through. In this way having a kind of second vacation.

3. A literary agent writes to say he's interested in representing my work. He wants to tell me about his clients, most of whom, he says, are professionals in one field or another. "There are medical doctors," he writes, "Ph.Ds, an Indian author who used to be a movie star, a lady veterinarian pilot who has spread her wings into adult mysteries, an eighty-five-year-young medical missionary with a wooden prosthesis leg (lost to gas gangrene in her early thirties) who has worked for over fifty years as a nurse in the remote regions of Northern India. There's a ... "

4. An organizer who has a German accent gives me details about an upcoming reading: "You will catch the three-thirty ferry. Dinner is served promptly at five-thirty. The reading begins at seven-thirty. You will read for forty-five minutes. Then there will be a lengthy coffee break after which you will read for another forty-five minutes. You will sleep on my couch. If you bring your husband he will sleep on the floor."

5. Driving to the town in southern Saskatchewan which has become famous as the home of junior hockey coach-pedophiles, the reading organizer tells me that there is one word I cannot say during my reading. "It's the four-letter word beginning with 'c' and ending with 't,'" he says. "They just cannot abide that word." I ask him if the four-letter word beginning with "f" and ending with "k" is all right. Also the seven-letter word beginning in "a" and ending in "e" which is used for rear end. "Are these words okay?" I wonder. These words, the organizer assures me, are fine: "There's no problem with them. But they'll walk out if you use the 'c' word."

6. After seeing me on a cable interview a woman acquaintance telephones. "You did very well," she tells me, "but I noticed that you used a lot of 'ums' and 'ahs.' I can help you with that. I'd like to invite you, as my guest, to the next meeting of Toastmasters International. It's at the Silver Threads. You go in the front door. But don't turn right. That's Bingo. Turn left." I instantly decide I love my "ums" and "ahs." I'll keep them. It's what saves me from sounding like I'm in sales.

7. After a reading I sleep in the home of a woman who is enamoured with angels. Small, glittery angel forms appear on tables, floors, countertops. They're everywhere like air freshener. There are also angel sayings placed here and there. On the sewing machine: *Every blade of grass has its own angel.* On the typewriter: *If everyone only listened to their angel.* On the bathroom mirror: *Make angel wings ten times.*

A large poster in the bedroom where I sleep is titled "How To Be An Artist." The poster lists several things I can do to become one: invite someone dangerous to tea; make friends with freedom; swing as high as you can on a swingset in moonlight; give money away; believe in magic; laugh a lot; take moon baths; draw on walls; giggle with children; play with stuffed toys; build a fort with blankets; hug trees.

The poster is colourful; there's an angel blowing a golden trumpet in each corner and the how-to instructions are printed against a large rainbow. A Care Bears ambiance hovers in the room. In the morning I flee. As I'm getting in my car, the woman calls gaily from the front steps, "You never know when you'll be touched by an angel!"

8. A book reviewer creates a prize. It's made out of an empty cereal box. He calls it the "Wet Salami." I am one of seven winners. It's possible I dreamt this. The winners are required to perform a musical number on stage; all of us wear identical blonde wigs. One of the winners plays the piano, the rest attempt a chorus line. I then step forward to deliver a speech of thanks. Looking back at the other winners I notice that they are all idiots, drooling sub-normals happy to be fêted. Each of us is holding a wet salami. One of the idiots is eating hers.

9. I give a reading before twenty-four empty black chairs. The reading goes well. There is nothing dreamlike about this occurrence. The reading goes well because I've given up all hope of an audience ever arriving; it's become clear that the twenty-four chairs have become my audience. I therefore conjure up significance: There is something exquisite about the way this double semicircle of chairs have hurled me into the moment, something ... er, wonderful ... about the way I've crashed into where I am. Which, on this rain lashed Wednesday evening in mid-December, is exactly nowhere, or as Donald Barthelme would say: nowhere—the exact centre.

10. At the last minute, my publisher changes the title of my new book to *All Chickens Are Sucks* and puts me in charge of promotion. This

may or may not be a dream. I take my duties seriously. At the book launch I wear a chicken outfit and sing in a chicken squawk the theme song from *Saturday Night Fever*: "Stayin' Alive." Then I read excerpts from the book. Every so often I let out a terrible chicken screech. For my finale I settle myself on the floor, grunt several times, and lay an egg. Everyone rushes for the book table. The publisher immediately begins a second printing.

DARWIN ALONE IN THE UNIVERSE
2003

GIFTS

I called for an early morning taxi and they sent a hearse. In a cunning effort to keep my mood black, I reasoned. A hearse. Making sure I got the point. But I got in. Liking the way the hearse idled in the driveway like a limousine. The way the uniformed driver opened the door, solicitous as an usher. Inside the hearse: music playing—Mozart's *Requiem* or it could have been Pink Floyd at Condo Hall. I sat in the front seat beside the driver feeling strangely buoyed: we were carrying no casket.

Travelling to the city, then, at a funereal pace. Noting the sober glances from passersby: a woman at an intersection with a look of heavy concern, a group of pensioners staring grimly. I smiled and waved, determined to be sunny.

Delivered at length to Forty-Fifth and Sharpe. There to walk the streets, my pockets full of dollar coins. To dispense at random to the squatting street kids with their dogs, sleeping bags, packs. And when a man asked for a cigarette I gave him the one I was smoking. And when a drunk holding an empty Listerine bottle said, "Spare change?" I gave him the rest of my coins. Thinking: whatever happened to Karl Marx?

Thinking: gifts. And the pigskin wallet that you in your downy life might possibly need. Visiting the warehouse where my old friend Mona practised supply side economics. In theory. Seven hundred pigs and a staff of twelve. The staff toiling third world fashion—strip, snip, toss. With a conveyer belt to the Chinese restaurant next door. The warehouse air chemically treated—made cool and sweet—

keeping the pigskins supple. Row upon row of skins hanging from lines like laundry.

And last week in the mail from the Bank of Commerce, another gift: Free Accidental Death Insurance to the tune of fifteen hundred dollars. For being a loyal consumer. What is this business of giving?

Choosing your wallet from the many pigskin items happily displayed. Buying wholesale. Thinking dear. Thinking: business might be a good way to go: simple rules and your nose aquiver with ad campaigns, market forces: your life reduced to yea or nay. And Mona to admire, a woman meaning business, with advice to give: *Oppose takeover bids. Prune your life of all things grey—sluggish partners and so forth.*

And will you admire your new wallet with its pouches greedy for your extra bills? Bought with wholesale intentions, mainly dear, love and so forth. And will my gift prove to be a wise investment? Thinking: whatever happened to Walt Whitman, that freewheeling champion of giddy days?

Propelling myself, then, to the afternoon reception where I paid homage to three floors of newly installed books. Keeping my mood on the far side of black. In theory. So many books. So little interest. Helped along in this endeavour by complimentary wine and sushi. Prowling the guests for advantage. And meeting Karen entertaining a crowd about Jack: *I got him straight from his mother and she practically wiped his ass. He doesn't know what helping is. Comes home, sits in front of the* TV, *plays with his computer. Gives me a face if I ask him to feed the dogs.*

Thinking: whatever happened to the Dalai Lama and the untainted, generous life?

Back on the streets. The sun shining in spite of itself. A city duly warmed. Imagining the pile-lined slippers I might possibly buy. Another gift. For your nightly TV vigil. Compounding my investment; my mood surging to bright. And will your feet in pile-lined slippers thank me? Your feet tender from years of giving your all: pounding pavements, carpets, linoleum, grass.

Meeting my friend Heather, then, for coffee at five dollars a pop. Coffee in theory. Made with chocolate, whipped cream, ad campaigns. The conversation turning to her lover, Ross: *They don't understand, do they? They don't consider* COMPLEXITY. *For them it's all business, the bottom line.*

Uh huh.

Thinking: intravenous Buddhism. Cleverly attached to our sleeping arms—subliminal brainwashing pumping us full of kindness, wisdom, love. And will the man asleep in the pet shop doorway thank me?

Thinking of what Sartre said: *There are two ways to go to the gas chamber, free or not free.*

Entering, then, the waiting hearse for my return trip home. Our newest form of public transportation, tailor-made for those of us preferring the slow, gloomy sweep, the funereal glide. The hearse taking me home. Where I'm a volunteer participant in whatever falls my way. Sometimes smiling, sometimes not.

And yesterday by mail a blessing from St. Mary's Church. With a special message from the churchwardens: *Please, we need your money.*

Giving and taking. Thinking: our ability to reconcile dark with light has diminished.

Filling out my coupon for a bag of microwave popcorn. Free with a fill-up at Save-On-Gas.

Intent on having giddiness.

DOWN THE ROAD TO ETERNITY

It's official. I've seriously decided to freeze my brain.

I couldn't wait to tell Mother. I was so excited I raced over to the Cormac McCarthy Retirement Commune, the place she co-founded for elderly freaks. She was in her room, beading another necklace. Cannabis smoke hung in the air like an incredibly hip deodorizer.

Once again I marvelled at how good Mother looked: tall and slim and tanned like an aged version of "The Girl from Ipanema." She was barefoot in her purple tie-dyed caftan; feathers and beads were twined through her long grey hair.

"Freezing brains!" I could hardly contain my glee. "It's the latest hope. Technology will make us eternal."

"Why go on suffering forever?" Mother asked, bored. "I thought the whole point was to end the cycle of birth and rebirth."

"That's your point, not mine," I said.

She closed her eyes and breathed deeply. "Again," she said, "what's the big deal about eternal?"

"Are you serious?" I screamed. "When you end your first life cycle, you get to have another one! Nanotechnology will make it possible. Scientists freeze your brain now, when you die, and then, when the technology's fully developed, they thaw it out. Just like that! In fifty years or five hundred. Then they grow a replacement body for your thawed out head. I want my next body to look like a twenty-four-year-old starlet."

Mother laughed so hard she choked.

I wrote in my journal: *It's official. I've seriously decided to freeze my brain.*

Why?

—Because my name is Willow, like a bad joke. I'm fat but not obese, chunky but not gross. I don't yet require two stools at a lunch counter.

—Because I'm thirty-one years old and was home-schooled in communes. I excel at playing in the woods and making God's Eyes out of wool and sticks. Try putting that on a resumé.

—Because the best job I can get is for minimum wage at Video Madness. My supervisor's a seventeen-year-old drug dealer named Conner who specializes in rave drugs, the speedy chemicals, buying empty gelatin capsules and filling them in the bathroom during his shifts. His pair of mongrels go everywhere with him. They're called Crystal and Meth.

—Because I live with a forty-year-old auto body repairman named Walter whose idea of enlightenment is watching plane crash marathons on TV. If only he could repair this body of mine.

—Because marijuana gives me anxiety attacks and meditation makes my nose bleed.

—Because I've searched for my bliss and found it was sleep.

—Because when I try to plump up my sagging self-esteem like it was a satin cushion there's nothing there to plump. My body may be thick but my inner life is as thin as a cracker.

—Because Mother says, "Call me Rayna!" her new name based on numerological principles. Before that she was Rose, then Athena, then

Starshine. Names based on something else, mythology, the zodiac, TV commercials.

So it's official. I've seriously decided to freeze my brain.

Mother's dying wish is to be stoned for the trip to the "Big Beyond." She says, "I want to go out like Aldous Huxley and be injected with acid. I don't want to face death with only this puny consciousness for company."

My dying wish is to get another life and avoid death altogether.

Mother says her final trip will be a mind fuck. I say fucking with my mind will be the least of it. It's my brain in a new body that I'm after. A new body meaning a new me. Don't believe the other hype. It really is the package that counts. Our brains will adapt. It'll be the ultimate makeover, a technological morph spanning centuries. Packed along with my frozen head will be a "before" picture of the ancient, flabby Willow which I'll look at from my fabulous new body for exactly ten seconds before ripping it to shreds.

Two hundred years from now the world will still go berserk over a beautiful woman. I'm counting on it. I want to be that woman. I have an Internet lover who thinks I'm that woman, now. His name is Donald Thomas and he's into freezing brains big time. Even though he says he's got a body like the star of *Tarzan*, even though he says he sells insurance and is obscenely rich, he's a dedicated man. He spends his free time fighting off the pessimists and trying to start a Movement.

Walter spends his free time lying on the couch in his boxer shorts and wife-beater T-shirt drinking beer and watching disaster shows. "Wilma!"—he calls me Wilma, like he was Fred and we're the Flintstones.

"Wilma, come see this!" And I'll go running and it'll be another boring killer tornado wrecking a trailer park.

Things are livelier with Donald. He believes my name is Kimmie. Cybernetic Kimmie is the first step towards the flesh and blood model existing somewhere down the road to Eternity.

Donald and me have what he calls "brain sex." That's the incredible thrill you get from the true linking of minds. So far he's been the only one getting the thrills because I don't understand half of what he says. But that's okay. I just play along being the blonde, willowy Slimmy Kimmy with the showgirl legs and the theoretically eye-popping breasts.

Dear Donnie

Thanks to you, it's official. I've seriously decided to freeze my brain. But are you sure it will work?

XO Your Blonde Bomber

Doll,

Thawing your brain out will be as easy as using a 23rd-century kid's chemistry set. And you know what? All those people waiting for a revival before they join the Movement will just have to die. Too bad.

Best and long, long life,

Donald

About freezing my brain, Mother said, "Why don't you freeze part of it now as a test run? The frontal lobes, for starters. We could use a hypo full of freezing compound and see what happens."

That's Mother. Always there for me with a bucket of ice water.

"You don't understand," I hollered. "You're a hopeless old hippie. Your time is past. Over. Finito. Everyone's doing pharmaceuticals now and watching videos and saving up for fifty-two-inch TV screens. Peace and love is a joke. High-tech is what's cool. And speed, and fashion, and being young and cutting edge. Which is what freezing brains is all about. Being cutting edge. Not old and mouldy like this commune."

"You don't know dick," Mother said, putting on her kind Buddhist voice, cozy as a homespun monk's robe.

She suggested I calm down and take her dog Smack for a walk. "Check out the new landscaping," she said. "It's done after Cormac McCarthy. I've always liked his writing. His reality's so sharp it cuts the skin."

"If you want your reality sharp," I said, "try surfing the Net and reading up on freezing brains. Freezing brains will leave Cormac McCarthy spitting dust."

But I took the dog anyway, passing in the hallway two macrobiotic old women. They were bald-headed and bent over, devotees of something or other.

When I got outside what I saw was drifts of sand and planted sagebrush. The place looked like a movie set of the old West. The only thing missing was a hot wind blowing beneath a blood meridian sky.

"Big deal," I told Smack. "Mother's created a theme park. A graveyard. Any minute now we'll see roving bands of bloodthirsty cowboys and Indians hacking one another to death with rifle butts and axes."

We climbed the dusty hill behind the commune and found a patch of newly grown moss to sit on. Nearby, a skinny old man wearing nothing but a pair of Jockey shorts was in the lotus position meditating.

"Excuse me," I called.

The man didn't move.

"Excuse me," I called again. "I just wanted to tell someone. It's official. I've seriously decided to freeze my brain."

He turned slowly and looked at me for a few moments before speaking. "Fuck off," he finally said.

Dearest Donnie,

When our brains are frozen will we have cozy side-by-side slots in cold storage?

XO Kimmie

Kim,

How many times have I told you? It's called Neuro Suspension!!! By the way, I sent you an insurance policy application form. Did you receive it?

Donald

Dusting the videos at work, I called over to Conner, "It's official. I've seriously decided to freeze my brain. Only I have to take out this life insurance policy and make the company the sole beneficiary. That's because freezing your brain costs so much money. Thousands and thousands of dollars."

Conner was behind the counter studying a spreadsheet about his drug business—scrunched face, Magic Marker in his hand. "What?" he said, turning down the master switch on the eight TV sets blaring cartoons. His nose ring vibrated, a sure sign he was choked. "Cool," he hissed when I told him again. "Whaaat Ev-eeeeer."

At home I said, "Hey, Walter, I've seriously decided … "

"Yeah, yeah … I know … to freeze your brain. It's another rip-off by insurance companies. Didn't you know that? They get people to take out huge insurance policies plus charge an annual holding fee. When you die, Wilma, they cut your head off, drain the blood, fill it with antifreeze, and put it in cold storage. Think about that! Then they burn the rest of you and flush your ashes down the toilet. With you it'll take several flushes."

"Very funny. But how'd you get so smart about the insurance companies?"

"Saw it on TV," Walter said. "Where else? On a show about future disasters. Freezing brains is some kind of idiot belief in future technology. Might as well believe in reincarnation. It's cheaper."

Dear Don,

Tell me again about Neuro Suspension. I'm getting kind of worried about the money.

Yours truly, Kimberly

Kimmie,

If you're cost conscious, the budget route is the best way to go. The death benefit on a hundred-thousand-dollar insurance policy will include, besides Neuro Suspension, cremation and burial of your non-frozen remains at sea. It's a bargain. But don't wait too long to act. There's so many people wanting this service that prices will be soaring within days. Kimmie, sign those forms now!

Yours in eternity, Don

I told a customer who was renting three adult videos. "It's official. I've seriously decided to freeze my brain."

The customer smirked at me, leering. "Frozen from the neck up. I like that. I like that very much."

I've told everyone I know. And everyone I don't know. Something's been decided. I'm seriously thinking. *Nanotechnology will make it possible.* It's official. The Girl from Ipanema will inject herself with acid. The Flintstones will watch disaster shows till death does them in. Cowboys and Indians will hack each other to death with rifle butts and axes. But something's been decided. The death benefit on a hundred-thousand-dollar insurance policy will ensure my survival. *Yours in long, long life.* I've seriously decided. When you end your first life cycle, you get another one. Mother laughed so hard she choked. *Thawing you out will be as easy as using a 23rd-century kid's chemistry set.* Adapt and live. Frozen from the neck up. A mind fuck a mind fuck. Donald Thomas, my lover, my sole beneficiary. *Stored at -179 degrees Celsius.* Willowy as a two-ton truck. Living forever in a beautiful starlet's body. It's official. My non-frozen remains will be flushed down the toilet. *Technology will make us eternal.* Wife-beater T-shirts, disaster shows on TV. Twentieth-century writer Cormac McCarthy wrote spare, gothic Westerns. Video Madness has over ten thousand videos in stock. I've seen them all. Something's been decided. My intuitive wisdom. My serious lack. My beautiful future. *Kimmie, sign those forms now!* The ultimate makeover. Blonde slimmy Kimmie with the eye-blinking breasts. Walter, Mother, Donald, Conner. Why would you want to live forever? Crystal and Meth. Grass and acid. It's cutting edge! It's Neuro Suspension! I'm so excited. It's official. Fuck off. I think I've seriously decided.

POINT TEN

1. TEN POINT LESSON

1. It is dangerous to be one half of a pair of lovebirds because lovebirds are enamoured of time. A lovebird is always trying to outlive its mate so it can pine away in exquisite grief. This is the prize: one dies so the other can sing.

2. There is a substance called oenanthic ether, which is found in the oxygen samples of those happily feasting on brotherly love. This ether may contain the antidote to brotherly strife.

3. Romantic love is a musical term meaning toccata and fumble. It is short-lived but can occur repeatedly in lives that are old, new, exotic, local, conventional or radical.

4. When love is lost do not be ashamed. Turn the memory of love on its side and push and pull and stroke it. Soon you will have a colourless, odourless shape like a glass dome, practical enough to encase your heart in.

5. When love is blind, meddle slowly and with care. Too much or too little inhabitancy will cause blind love to miss its mark and you'll be left holding the donkey's tail.

6. The love knot is supposedly an interlaced bow made of ribbon but lovers know it as that sated realm where to even utter a tender word is too exhausting.

7. Love Lies Bleeding and Bleeding Hearts are the names of plants and, while suitable as nineteenth century metaphors for a broken heart, they are too sentimental for our cooler times. Choose metaphors that are pest-free and ultra-hardy, ones that prefer wasteland environs such as shopping malls, concrete boulevards, airports, abandoned king-sized beds.

8. The cure for love sickness is a tasty bit of anything forbidden such as a Black-Thorn cocktail made of Irish whiskey, French vermouth, absinthe and Angostura bitters.

9. If Platonic love heats up dangerously, set up an immediate chill. The secret of a quick and gentle exit is plenty of idealism; no one wants to be accused of upsetting the story.

10. In games, love scores nothing.

2. TEN POINT DEFENSE

1. A person's original nature attracts or repels certain wisdoms; hence no expert can with assurance affirm that any particular wisdom is better than another.

2. The earliest records of wisdom almost uniformly refer to it in connection with religious celebration, i.e., the effect on the brain.

3. There is no substantial evidence that wisdom has contributed to the corruption of mankind, other than in connection with evangelism, which, being an emotion, is a brain by-product.

4. A frequently asked question: Where does the pursuit of wisdom lead its devotees? A common answer: To laurels and hindsight, most certainly, to the harmless and delightful thrill of a wise and moderate wit.

5. The combining and manipulating of nature's more potent thoughts should not be treated as a mere matter of routine. Devils of confusion are lurking everywhere. They're only too happy to caricature importance and to spoil polite Socratic events.

6. It is prudent to remember that households in all parts of the world are engaged in their own brand of tragicomedy, all of them excellent.

7. To the nervous who may seek wisdom without understanding there lurks potential gloom: *mal de mer* and headache may substitute for a planned and happy affair with life.

8. To a normally healthy person there is a fair certainty that some wisdom, taken with forbearance and in postmodern fragments, will contribute materially to the health of the species.

9. It is always a wise decision to suspend definitive judgment on any matter at all.

10. As an added bonus, wisdom acts as a mild stimulant on the adult orgasm and is a solvent for pasty accusations concerning performance in that sphere, sweetie pie, my beloved.

3. TEN POINT TOUR

1. Seduced by *sang-froid* we rode the city streets in busses made of bulletproof metaphysics. The busses had clear, indestructible platinoid instead of glass for the windows. Outside: car lights and casualties.

2. Many things have absorbed then dulled our interiors so that now it takes a violent swizzle to renew the deadly. Never mind, we say, trusting the next stereotype, the next expression of mind. Never mind.

3. We are damaged, but brilliantly. See how our scars weep music.

4. Riding the busses, we felt sad about our lives, that short stretch between black and black where we don the clothes of the world, disguising ourselves as wonders.

5. Riding the busses, we prowled our nihility like tourists.

6. Years ago nothing could touch us. We were safe from the mazurka of inner-city mayhem. Snapping our fingers we let our heavens collide, as in love! Years ago we were imparadised! Married to a tour bus of our own making.

7. Now, passing the pink and white bodies of newborn animals left for dead by the side of the road, you said, "This is what happens when a civilization turns off meat, when animal flesh is reviled," and a man seated across from us nodded his head and said, "Ironic, isn't it?"

8. As ever, there are many slides into sediment and we never know which moment will contain an earthquake. This is our song. We sing about our lucky escapes.

9. Still, I pointed out the window: "Look! A parade!" The bus slowed and the crowd on the sidewalk cheered. A wedding procession sped by.

10. We felt—metaphysically speaking—happy.

4. A

1. Trundolatry. The worship of change. Much easier to live with.

2. A new practice, yes. Relatively speaking. With a bunch of improvements you can't see. Like the notion of time. You don't get stuck in the long-term. Diversion remains intact.

3. Agreed. The word worship is a problem. More it's the belief about what's great. An exaltation of the short-term.

4. Well, that's difficult to say. But essentially it's the rapid wearing out of interest. That's the idea behind it. As the moment changes so does the interest.

5. True. But somehow the moment defines itself. You don't have to think about it. Just ride the bus. Check out the view. There are lots of moments and lots of interests. Take your pick.

6. You could say that. But what's the problem with surface? It's a fast ride so you have to skim. Everything's on the menu.

7. Whatever floats your boat.

8. The usual things. Any kind of star. Sometimes food, a colour, a country. Sometimes yourself. There's no telling.

9. Well, we just stop paying attention. We move on. There's nothing mysterious …

10. True, again. But interest in this communication is fading. There's something else …

5. TEN POINT WEIGHT

1. I heard the cry of agitated crows and shielded my eyes, peering at the sky for reasons. A turkey vulture, black and red beaked, was attacking a crow's nest in a nearby tree. From the crows came a terrible cry of panic. Higher up, a pair of eagles lazily drifted.

2. At the same time, an ambulance backed out of the yard next door, discreetly removing the body.

3. You said, "Did you know that eagles mate for life?" and this thought gave me comfort.

4. It was the same comfort I felt at a party while watching a woman with a bottle of Echinacea dispense twenty drops into her husband's martini. She had the look of a zealot, dead serious, humourless. She said, "I've personally taken charge of Bob's immune system."

5. You cringed and headed for the drinks table.

6. But I faced a wall and cried. After twenty-six years, which in married terms is a lifetime, I'd take charge of your immune system, too, if you'd let me. Take charge like it was a medieval fortress and I was Captain of the Guards throwing spears and fireballs at bacteria, multiplying cells, attacking hearts, killer thoughts.

7. But you don't believe in invisible things, refusing to prostrate yourself before another description of doom. "The immune system!" you declared. "Who dreamed up that metaphor?"

8. When the ambulance removed the body of our neighbour, a cry of panic settled mutely in my chest like a twenty-six-pound weight dragging me closer to you but down, as well.

9. When the time comes, death offers a shopping mall of possibilities, from small deaths to large. Everyone knows this. But who amongst

us is not tempted by a final, gaudy flourish? Some give away their money, hoping for a monument. Some become hysterically kind in an eleventh-hour bid to curry favour. This much is observable.

10. And this. It is early June, warm and bright. The pink climbing roses are in full bloom along the side of the house. The lawns are still green. There's a strong breeze coming in from the sea. And poplar leaves are snapping like flags at a fair.

THE HEARTSPEAK WELLNESS RETREAT

After the guests had left we did, you know, Feng Shui. We had this book, *Instant Feng Shui*, that did away with the three thousand years it takes to understand the practice and made it, well, instant. Feng Shui has to do with energy flow and balance and harmony and it had just been discovered in the West. It's the latest ancient thing. And this book, *Instant Feng Shui*, boiled the practice down to a few handy how-to's which we appreciated, being on the short side of a three-thousand-year-old tradition. The book had a checklist called "Tips for Serenity" which was a kind of fast track to cosmic understanding and this was another thing we appreciated.

Feng Shui is this ancient Asian practice, a very old practice, we understood, even more ancient than Moses or the Greeks. The most ancient practice there is, practically ground zero as far as enduring, ancient practices go. More ancient than stone worship by the Druids which, when you think about it, was really just a bunch of people in good-looking hooded robes staring at boulders and getting cold at the sunrise.

So we consulted *Instant Feng Shui* after the guests had left their, you know, negative karma about the place, their critical, snotty comments and their foul moods making it difficult for us to sleep and generally carry on in the elevated, serene way we'd been so diligently practising.

The guests, a pair of hefty, middle-aged sisters from Winnipeg— nylon leisure suits, brush cuts—had rented the suite sight unseen from our ad in *Nature Now!* It was the first ad for our suite, renamed

The Heartspeak Wellness Retreat—: "Experience the life-enhancing calm ... "—and the sisters were our first guests.

On the second day of their three-week stay they began complaining. Where was the ozone-filtered water? What was Eco-friendly about a track house set in the suburban wilderness behind a strip mall? And where, they demanded, with three noisy preteens in residence, was the calm?

Soon after they began directing their malevolent energy towards us from below. We could actually feel it invading our sacred meditation time like a seeping mould. It took the form of chills and crankiness and black-hearted nastiness amongst the upstairs inhabitants—Jason and the boys, the household pets, myself. We could actually, you know, experience our perfect Now being contaminated. The sun may have shone for the time the guests were with us but their souls were imprisoned in a permanent thundercloud.

The dog's vicious dislike of the guests was their fault, of course; animals know and despise negative beings. Ditto for the droppings left by the cat on their kitchen floor. The suite's repeatedly overflow-ing toilet, the rips in the sheets, and the rock thrown through their bedroom window were further examples of the negative attracting the negative. About the broken window, we're certain it was not caused by one of our boys. More likely it was a message from a large, rock-hurling eagle and doesn't that speak volumes? Eagles, as everyone knows, are emissaries, ancient emissaries from the spirit world and they always make an appearance when negative forces are at the boil.

It's a blessing, I told Jason, that the guests paid for the rental in advance. It was an even greater blessing when they cut short their visit by ten days and moved to a motel in the city. Their names were Arlene and Bonnie and they left in a huff. I tried practising Tonglen while they loaded their rented Mazda. I tried practising Tonglen very hard. I stood on the front porch, screwed shut my eyes, breathed deeply, and concentrated on sending wave upon wave of loving kindness to those red-faced beings. Any time you encounter blood-boiling rage, Tonglen is the kindest thing you can do. Never give irritating paying guests a refund.

After they'd roared out of the driveway flinging gravel everywhere we meditated for thirty minutes. Then we consulted *Instant Feng Shui*. The book told us how to cleanse our home after unwelcome visitors have left. First you put two heavy stone jars on either side of the front door to usher in new beginnings. Then you light firecrackers. Set off firecrackers in the places where the offending guests have been. And this setting off of firecrackers made sense to us. Tiny explosions clearing the air, shaking things up, restoring harmony. Throw open the windows, the book advised, and light about two dozen firecrackers, mainly in doorways and in places where the guests have slept. And violà!, the book promised, clarity and peace restored.

But we encountered this big problem. It was mid-August and just try buying firecrackers in mid-August. There's some law against it. Some law that says you can only buy firecrackers during the last two weeks of October, for Hallowe'en. So we wondered, what now? Because our need was pressing—bad karma headaches, pictures falling off the walls, general imbalance and disharmony in our home, the human and pet inhabitants gnawing on one another's tranquility.

So we built a bomb. Five bombs actually. Five little bombs trying, you know, to approximate firecracker size. But, of course, this was difficult. Jason and I visited Home Hardware for the raw ingredients, the dynamite and fuses and something to put the bomb-making materials into—tubing, we decided, plastic or metal tubing. And we encountered difficulty in the form of suspicious looks from the hardware store clerks who seemed to be thinking, you know, that we were dangerous, and while we'd certainly be the first to admit that there's plenty of things to be dangerous about these days, animal testing being a major scandal in our opinion and generally, the abuse and neglect of cats and dogs, well, this was not one of those times.

I said to Jason, after receiving a blast of ill wind from the pinch-mouthed clerk while purchasing bulk dynamite and filling out all those forms, I said, what we need to do right now, right here is Light Body. That's when you imagine, you know, a protective white light surrounding your body. So we did that. We said to the clerk, "Excuse us!" ran outside to the parking lot, got in our car, and practised Light Body. We got comfortable on the front seat—shoes off, lotus position—and took several deep abdominal breaths. We then visualized a protective white light emanating from the tips of our skulls and surrounding our bodies, top to bottom, side to side, like an egg.

When we returned to the hardware store inside our newly created, shimmering eggs everything was serene and delightful. In no time we completed our purchases.

Jason later said in affirmation, "You know, while I was practising Light Body it was amazing. A red light travelled all the way up from my perineum to my sixth Chakra where it became the most beautiful purple colour."

Jason, formerly in real estate, formerly called Gerald, followed his bliss last year and now does ear coning for a living. "I can't explain it," he's often said of his transformation, "but I felt this overwhelming call for ear wax and candles, for helping people with sinus irritation and tinnitus. I feel like I've got a Date with Destiny."

For a fee he'll also read your aura. So when he tells you he sees purple he means purple. Thanks to meditation, yoga, ozone therapy, Touch point reflexology, zero-balancing, his Shamanic drumming circle, and a Vegan diet, Jason's become a mild, pony-tailed, teddy bear of a man and all the women, his clients, just love "Ears by Jason."

He's funny, too, but in a joyful, non-judgmental way. When everyone started doing Random Acts of Kindness, Jason, for some reason, misunderstood the word "kindness," the way you can misread a headline and get a completely different meaning. He started doing Random Acts of Kinkiness and, for several days, handed out condoms and yellow nylon rope to complete strangers. While sharing with me the hostile reactions he'd received, I discovered his error.

"I don't understand it," he said, mystified. "Handing out all those condoms and ropes, I really believed I was touching people's hearts, rekindling our oneness, our kindred spirits. It felt wonderful."

What also felt wonderful was our successful practice of Feng Shui to rid our home of the bad karma left by the guests. Our homemade firecrackers, our mini-bombs, were each about the size of a Cuban cigar. For safety's sake, we made sure that each one had a fuse long enough to travel from inside the suite to the far end of the back yard. There, the boys and Jason and I gathered in a healing circle to ask for the Earth Goddess's blessing before lighting the fuses. And when those bombs exploded our relief was instant. Peace and harmony just came flooding back into our home like from an unleashed dam. We were so overjoyed we danced in spinning, you know, cosmic circles around the back yard—Jason and me, the boys, the dog.

The municipal firefighters, when they arrived with their sirens screaming, were amazed that there's been so little damage—only one window broken and some incidental burn holes in the bedding. Otherwise there was just this pervasive, healing, sulphur-smelling smoke everywhere.

A month later that smell was still with us working its Feng Shui magic. That is, until we received a registered letter from Wisdom Inc., the company in Phoenix, Arizona that was giving Jason and me our correspondence course in Enlightenment. It was the letter we'd been waiting for. Although we know we're supposed to live without fear or hope, we couldn't help feeling disappointed by the letter's contents.

We'd taken the course, completing all the chapters, writing the tests, pondering the red-inked replies, and redoing some of the questions, as required. We took it all very seriously. Then, when the final exam had been written, we filled out the application form for Graduate Postings, hoping for some exotic background in which to parade our newly awakened selves. Our passports were in order; we'd designated a Power of Attorney, and packed our bags. In short, we did everything that was required, including finding foster homes for the boys.

Now came the reply: Overseas posting denied. Candidates insufficiently evolved. Recommendation: Stay where you are. Take another course. Better luck next time.

We were stunned. We'd been posted to our own back yard.

Jason was momentarily, you know, livid. He'd been hoping to practice ear coning internationally. He started seeing red everywhere and not the good kind of red, either. "I'm forty-nine years old!" he cried. "I paid all that money to go through all those bleeding levels and I have to remain here?"

"Maybe it's a test," I said. "Some kind of ultimate test."

"What isn't ultimate?" he snapped.

"Exactly."

We unpacked our bags.

Temporarily, for a nanosecond of my emptied Now state of mind, I was disillusioned. I was having misgivings about the Human Potential Movement and nearly changed my name from Ambika Crystal, Divine Bodywork Pet Counsellor, back to Debbie Thornbur, preparer of income tax returns.

Fortunately, *Instant Feng Shui* was on hand with its sage advice. "To promote happiness and prosperity and to hasten your journey along the path to Enlightenment," I read, perhaps a little too anxiously, "place a clear glass paperweight before a mirror in your hallway. At the exact same time each day, stand before the mirror and place your hands on the paperweight. Now, with shoulders relaxed and head erect, gently smile at your reflection. Keep smiling for forty-five minutes. Do this for twenty-seven days."

This has now become my principal daily practice. While awaiting results, I've been writing in my "Vision Journal" as instructed by the knowing people at Wisdom Inc. Our first assignment for the new course is this: We are to imagine that the house we've lived in for eleven years with the boys, the dog and cat and assorted possessions, is entirely New. We are to experience each moment with awakened eyes, as if the next moment after that will be one of blindness, deafness and/or sudden, violent death.

This is what I wrote this morning:

Daybreak. Light frost. Sky along the strip mall washed pink and grey. Brushstroke of cloud stretching east to west. I, Ambika Crystal, a human haiku in a velour dressing gown, am throwing toast crusts from an upstairs window to the scavenging crows in the backyard below. The cat sits at the side of the lawn, her jaws vibrating at the sight of the birds. Oh, get on with it, kill the bloody things, I want to scream. And scream.

Startled by what I had written, I raced back to the mirror. A double dose of Feng Shui should help.

Now I'm smiling. And for added measure, chanting "Ohmm-mmm." Smiling and chanting at the same time is not as difficult as it sounds. Try this when the journey's not moving along, you know, fast enough.

BRAVE NEW DESIRES

We wrenched the show away from Hemingway. Talked the reaction out of Parker's handle. Were walking by when Arbus hurled herself from a nine-volt battery. She fell on us but lived to create a *pièce de résistance*.

Plath required a stone casket. We hired an army of contrarians and sealed every dormer in the vicinity of her enormity. All Joplin required was conveyancing. Look, we told her, we'll make sure Everyman loves you; you can end your romance with pilots and borders.

Van Gogh needed perverting but in the end was grateful for our dialectic; he found it calming to know his vision was disturbed. When Poe barricaded himself inside his campaign, we slipped a pistol through his campaign door, begging him to give the worst another tsunami.

Soon afterward we filed a warrant and listed whitening, flight, hostesses, rosaries and rules as the usual suspicions. We locked evolution away.

Woolf was the hardest. We waited at her sickness for years and when the time came, hauled her away from the cerebral. It's because of her we eradicated all seams.

Seams are brave new desires now—horizons, separations, shape.

Darwin Alone in the Universe

The fire at the Drop-In Yoga Centre was quickly brought under control. There were a few moments of fire-fighting heroics, then it was over. Then it was back to normal, back to the soup, back to the personal cop show. Your good guys, your bad guys. Your bang bang bang.

This is a picture of the smoke rising above the torched Centre. Afterwards, questions were raised; yoga instructors were filmed for the *Late Breaking News*. But the real value of the fire occurred during its burning. Because something specific had happened, a counterpoint, a clarifying bas-relief. Like what happens when a plane crashes or a murder is committed. The event jumps out *specifically* from the background chaos, the focus enlarges, and the wider world is seen. Illuminated.

My name is Darwin, like the man who invented the monkey. I hit the planet in '59. I was named Darwin because 1959 was the centenary of the publication of *The Origin of Species*. My father, now dead, was a postal clerk whose hobby was botany. He was also a vegetarian and an atheist, the only one in the neighborhood, or as I came to understand from the school taunting I received, the only one in the world. I spent my childhood being singled out for weirdness. Like my father, I'm a loner. I regard this fact as an extreme form of random good luck.

My last trip to the hospital was in '91. I thought something was controlling me. I was right. It was my own mind.

Being crazy is being the victim of mind-fuck situations all the time.

In the hospital I was pinned down and questioned by behaviourist nerds. I fought back. I told them I'd look after my own mental health. Then I discovered Freud and psychoanalyzed myself. This is what I learned: maintaining clarity in the waking state is the most difficult thing of all. Maintaining illumination, next to impossible. But I followed Freud's example and, giving myself repeated raps to the mindset in much the same way a jackhammer pulverizes cement, I was able to successfully eliminate a large portion of my unconscious mind. Now I never dream. And my emotions have become mere passing phenomena.

These things I have done in order to avoid the pharmaceutical control of the mental health militia.

For some of us, these *are* the dark ages.

But I'm not dangerous.

Do you sense the agitation? It's everywhere, but especially in the cities. The inhabitants there are restless, over-stimulated, desperate to maintain a transient vital energy. They shop, eat, drink, watch videos, ravenously. Everyone's wild-eyed, nervous, catwalking through crowds and traffic like haunted runway models. Pacing the streets, nerve endings vibrating. Money in their pockets, fulfillment eluding.

Everyone's hungry. Most hungry are the images that hold us in thrall—the images that sell us things, that entertain us. Who would have guessed that this is what artificial intelligence has become: visual images with lives of their own feeding on *our* hunger?

The whole world has become a madness machine.

Your so-called "advanced civilization."

I know. I'm just another angst-ridden Postmodern casualty.

Easily dismissed.

Bang. Bang.

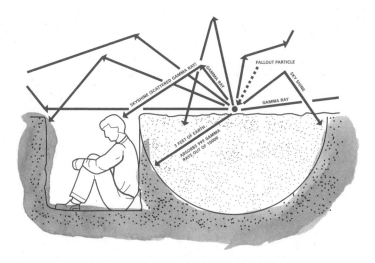

This is a picture of me in my trench.

In my mother's backyard in the city. When I built it she was happy. "It's just like when you were a boy with your Erector set in the basement," she said.

She was wrong. When I was a boy I was filled with a wild and ultimately stupid hope, creating the elaborate and beautiful metal forms of a skeleton city.

Now I dig holes.

When you abandon hope you also abandon hopelessness.

But I've discovered that an open trench provides poor protection. The slings and arrows of skyshine and gamma rays; the pounding music from the giant ad screens mounted on city buildings; the jarring wail of ambulance and police sirens sound like a city screaming in pain.

These things penetrate the fragile brain.

Speaking of brains, did you know that somehow the water of the physical brain is turned into the wine of consciousness? But that scientists draw a blank on the nature of this conversion? The concept is simple. It's like watching a white trail in the sky (brain) tracking the movement of a supersonic jet (consciousness).

Even with the penetrating rays and noises, I'm relaxed in my trench. Relief washing over me as I watch the white trail disappear.

Once I sat on the curbs of busy streets writing poems about anguish, love and terror. Some people still do that. Huddle inside their lives dragging pens across their pain.

The world is filled with inexplicable things. And love is in hiding. Perhaps this has always been so and it's just that now we have too much black information, our perception has become damaged. Narrowed. Warped. Listen to the headlines; they say it all: "*There is a great panic amongst the people and they have spilled out into the streets."* ... *"Corpses are piled on verandas. Bruised and bleeding bodies are laid in rows along the streets ...* "

The information is all like this.

But information is not understanding.

Darwin provided a glossary at the end of *The Origin of Species*. The word *degradation* is listed: *the wearing down of land by the action of the sea or of meteoric agencies.*

Change a couple of words and you've got Darwin Two's definition of the times: *Degradation: the wearing down of the human species by the action of negative information.* Or read the OED: *Degradation: to become degenerate; a morbid change in structure.*

Mother barricades herself inside her home. Most people do. Her trust in a beneficent world has become *degraded.* "You want my opinion?" Mother whispers through the bolted door. "Everything hurts! Inside. Outside. Everything is shattering like glass."

Citizens tearing their hair, uncomprehending.

The cities are terrible places to live.

This is a sentence I like: There is newer and stronger evidence that the solitary individual who has disconnected himself from Postmodern life may actually represent the last vestige of independent, human thought.

A glimmer, a *modus operandi*, a casual illumination, perhaps.

Perhaps, even, the species *value* of Postmodern dislocation. A thing not easily dismissed.

Newer and stronger. Isn't that what the original Darwin was all about?

Still, I vacillate. Who knows anything for sure? Who even understands?

This is a picture of my unconscious mind. It's black, as in, empty. It's like a night scene in a city without lights. Something is there but you can't see it. It's like willed, internal blindness. The interior barely existing. This is a view that spiritual people the world over aspire to. In the picture I've left three stars shining. These represent points of connection. They allow for the occasional moment of spontaneity. I had one of those a few years ago. I jumped off a cliff into the ocean. It was great.

Ha. Ha.

That was a joke.

Something I'm still capable of.

Here's another joke.

During a lifetime, a couple of things might happen to make you laugh. But usually you're stuck on your back at the bottom of some trench, the world sitting on your face like some obnoxious fat man using your head for a pillow.

Did I say, "joke"?

Jump shot to right about now. I thought I'd build a better shelter. I found an old book about nuclear war. Now there's nostalgia. The comfort of a single external threat. None of this vague, confusing stuff. But a clear, constant menace, something you could get your teeth into.

So this book. From the survivalist movement of the early eighties. The cover: large black letters on a gunmetal grey background. Inside: a revelation of practical instructions. How to ventilate and cool a below-ground shelter. Emergency sanitation. Surviving without doctors. Improvised clothing. Air pumps. Water and Food: *In the histories of great famines, some people do rob and kill for food, and a very few become cannibals. But the big majority continues to maintain civilized values while they starve.* Self-Defence: *There is no need to tell people that they will need their guns ...*

The book had everything, even personal stories. A family of six from Utah travelled sixty-four miles by car to a remote countryside location and built a door-covered trench shelter in only thirty-four hours. A pair of college girls made a hose ventilated toilet out of a five-gallon paint can. Three rural families in Tennessee built an expedient blast shelter in forty-eight hours complete with bunks and bed sheet hammocks. A man travelled fifteen miles on foot carrying eighty pounds of water in two burlap bags, each lined with two plastic trash bags.

I decided on a Small-Pole Shelter.

Tools required to build a Small-Pole Shelter:

Axe, long handle.

Bow-saw, 28 in.

Pick.

Shovel, long handle.

Claw hammer.

File, 10 in.

Steel tape, 10 ft.

The beauty of a plan: the particular in sharp focus. This may be the secret of a smooth existence, the pathway to a temporarily untroubled life.

A Small-Pole Shelter provides excellent protection against fallout radiation, blast, and fires. Twelve people can live in this shelter without serious hardship. For Darwin Two it's a palace.

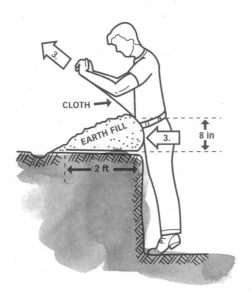

This is a picture of me building the Small-Pole Shelter.

A picture I've titled, "A lonely, intelligent mutation scrambling with the brutes for existence."

À la Darwin One. Who also worried about being seen as a monomaniac or a crank.

Darwin alone in the universe.

Here are some questions.

1. What if evolution has for some reason speeded up like a generalized cancer and that a rapid species change is occurring? That what once took millions of years to transmute and evolve is now taking one or two generations? That we are now fundamentally different animals from what our grandparents were?

2. What if all the lone, discontented, dismissed and hated voices living on the edge of our species' existence are really an aberration, a mutation?

3. What if independent, objective thought is the cause of this mutation? Has, in fact, *become* the mutation?

4. What if the song we mutants should be singing starts like this: *Hey Mama, I'm extinction bound ...*

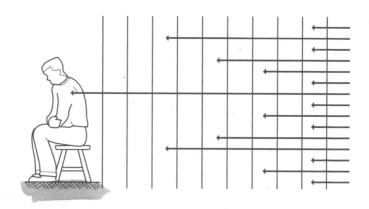

Another picture, this one of me resting. The Small-Pole Shelter half complete.

Then came Dorothy like a random variation hauling her busted rainbow. Wandering the universe, homeless, deviating, stunned. Stopping by my half-built shelter. I told her to take off, get lost. But she was already lost. She stayed and after a few days made a nest for herself against my mother's fence. A green plastic tarp crudely fashioned into a lean-to, a ratty sleeping bag.

Dorothy. Named for the 1939 film, carrying the burden of Oz: an alien world of delight and menace, magic and loyal friends.

Now that's a definition of *extinction*.

Dorothy who seldom speaks.

A kid, in her early twenties. Spending her days clearing bits of wood from the shelter site, hauling dirt, tidying up. Seeping slowly into my life.

During this time I still slept and ate in my mother's house. I started leaving her food like the stray animal she was.

Weeks went by. I became accustomed to her quiet presence. She'd watch me work on the shelter, helping when she saw the need. When the shelter was complete, I invited her inside. She moved her things to a far corner, away from my bunk. We are not lovers; we seldom speak, we never touch. But Dorothy has become my apprentice.

"Variation Under Domestication." This is the title of Chapter 1 of the *Origin*.

Dorothy. An allied species.

This is a picture of Dorothy and Darwin Two—in disguise, of course—resting in the Small-Pole Shelter the morning after the Multiplex Cinema burned down. A spectacular fire lasting throughout the night and spreading to neighbouring buildings. Several of the mounted ad screens were also destroyed, a hugely fulfilling sight: blue and white electrical sparks exploding from the screens as they burned, the prancing images and the music suddenly eliminated, the blank screens crashing to the ground.

Did I say I wasn't dangerous? I may have lied. Independent thought or action is always dangerous.

Illumination, of any sort, is dangerous.

And fire, in particular, can be cleansing.

THE WHITE SATIRE

The bride's dress was beautiful. It was made of white satire and flowed about her in an elegant trample.

The wedding ceremony took place on a revolving stair and was conducted by the lead guitarist of a local rock group. Afterwards, the groom bowed and the bride did a ballerina curtsy. The audience was huge and everyone applauded. But the groom had had enough by then and became slack and cold. Now the bride saw him as a thin and sour manager. The man in her mind had fled!

A dear friend stepped in and became the stand-in groom. Together they greeted the guests. There was no harm in this. Everyone thought the stand-in was the groom.

As for the real groom, he was never seen again.

"What lucre!" cried the bride.

Now she gives talks on wedding preparations to dazed young wits. They all want a white satire like hers.

"White satires are essentially harmless and delightful," the bride tells them. "Setting is important, of course, but anything loose will do—a hallucination, the great outrageous. A reluctant groom is useful for the photographs but if one isn't available, a stand-in will do. After that … pfft! And make sure the minister is novel."

The young wits are taking notes. "Reluctant groom," they write. "Novel!" "Hallucination!" "Outrageous!" "Delight!"

CHEERLEADING

During the birthday dinner—there was just the two of them—
they talked about art and how the "new" music seemed to be
leading the arts as far as expressing the present time was concerned—
the bass driven DJ compositions, almost symphonic in their construction,
yet elemental, heart pounding. How this music delighted and excited
while expressing a seamless present! Music subtly layered, full of
unpredictability and surprise. At the time they were listening to St.
Germain's *Boulevard* and drinking red Bordeaux.

Still thinking of music, she mentioned the notion that consciousness is tied to technology, that, historically, consciousness has changed
alongside technology. "Or probably," she said, "it is that they are
paired, each influencing and altering the other."

Briefly, they imagined a "Minuet mind," pinched and decorous,
then a "Christian mind," trapped in its own narrative, a "Gutenberg
mind," which must have been initially frightening, a "Digital mind,"
embryonic, confusing.

The writer J.G. Ballard was mentioned next, and his statement
that, contrary to popular perception, the twentieth century was not
dominated by holocaust and doom but was, in fact, a century of
optimism and naiveté. They thought about that for a while and
wondered if perhaps human beings have a cheerleader gene, as a kind
of survival mechanism, hidden away in their DNA makeup.

They considered the societal function of inspiration—uplifting
thoughts and feelings. Perhaps there was some basic drive to
exaltation, he suggested, the whole purpose being to provide a parallel

experience to the bleak facts undermining human existence. A deeper and more lasting perspective, say, than religion or entertainment provided. Many, they agreed, were whole-heartedly, and by definition singly, engaged in this endeavour. Artists and fevered scientists caught unawares in an unlikely union like good news ambassadors for the race, all of them desperate to find the cure for the human condition.

They went for a walk, the evening lengthening now in early April. The air was sharp, the sky overcast but lovely with many small birds chattering in the leafless poplars, and the dangling flower cones of the maple trees shedding their fine yellow dust on the roadway, on their shoulders.

On the beach thousands of seagulls perched on the rocks and many flew overhead in cawing agitation. It was said that after fifty years the herring had, inexplicably, returned to the inlet. Suddenly their neighbourhood beach had become a feeding ground. There were other birds, too, ravens, and more crows than they'd ever seen amassed at one place. And many bald eagles. When the eagles flew above the rocks, the perched gulls rose in one fluid movement; they were the exact same colour as the grey sky.

After the beach they walked home and she made coffee. He presented a small birthday cake—vanilla with a cream and wafer filling. Today she was fifty-one years old. But there was only one lit candle on the cake, a stub end from the sideboard, and she blew it out and made a wish which concerned the continuing good health of their children. The talk then settled on their children, especially in light of the birthday wish, and of the framed pictures of them he'd given her as a gift.

Admiring the gift she remarked that while the children were living at home, they'd never showcased their pictures—other than snapshots on the fridge—and how it was strange but also sad to see them mounted now, their images like ghosts or spirits hovering around them.

And so the evening continued. Still seated at the table, they turned their gaze outward once more, towards the world, and watched the moon rise, and listened to the birdsong outside. They found it surprising and lovely to hear birdsong while the moon shone.

THE AIR IS THICK WITH METAPHORS

We'll score the winning goal, capture the grand slam, ace the hole-in-one. After that, in the Pairs Free Dance, we'll execute a perfect triple salchow, a transcending move so unexpectedly pure that simultaneous orgasms will occur amongst those watching, perhaps millions of them.

We'll change our names to Cheeky and Markita and clean up in the Latin category of Ballroom Dancing in America. The crowd will love our sleek and piquant moves, our predatory Salsa, the way you push and pull me with your hot, animal eyes.

We'll shake champagne bottles and, ecstatic, pour the contents over each other's heads. This will be on the podium after the Indy win, after the sudden death playoffs, after the gold medals, after the successful births of our children, after the successful birth of anything.

We'll pose nude for *National Geographic*, part of a special feature titled, "Undiscovered Lovers of the Pacific West Coast." Following this we'll appear on the cover of the Canadian Tire catalogue in a tribute to long-term domesticity. You'll be cooking hamburgers from a dazzling silver barbeque and wearing a brilliant grin. I'll be wearing slim suburban slacks and smiling demurely while serving plates of food to Grandma and the kids. The sun will be shining. There won't be dangerous shadows anywhere.

During long summer evenings we'll give dinner parties for our friends with which we'll celebrate everything, moment by dissolving moment. Over candles and our favourite French Merlot. We'll watch the watercolour sunset. "Look!" we'll say, "the air is thick with metaphors!" This phrase will haunt us with its multiplicity of meanings, for years.

We'll do commercial endorsements for rare and thrilling music, especially cello solos that break your heart, and for golden retrievers, which also break your heart. In fact, we'll endorse rare and thrilling passion in a big way. Even while scrubbing the soup pot, even while buying dog food.

Together, like gladiators, we'll battle six-hundred-pound poetic chickens, reminding each other that so much depends upon the white chickens, the red wheel barrow, the rain, and on their enormous breasts which, when metaphorically cut up and stir fried, will feed a dinner party of thousands. After the meal we'll run the hundred-metre dash, breaking through the finish line together, arms secure around each other's waists, laughing, coming first.

We'll pretend we're a species apart and, like anthropologists, stalk couples that are dressed alike. Hanging out of car windows or climbing portable aluminum ladders, we'll sneak up on them in streets or in restaurants, shrieking together over a rare shot. Then we'll fill a gallery with our pictures, calling the show "Fusion." Thousands of couples will come to look at themselves, or couples like them, on the gallery walls. Afterwards they'll leave smiling, feeling pleasantly confirmed. There'll be beige couples, and blue couples, and plaid couples with rakish matching tams. On a wall by itself will be our prize photo, a really interesting blonde pair. Our self-portrait.

We'll inhabit each other's erotic dreams, kissing in doorways like hungry strangers, lips wet and full. Then we'll run away together, to this house, this very house, where we'll live nattily ever after.

We will call it love.

THE BREAKDOWN SO FAR
2007

Now is the Time

The Christian roofer has been phoning us for six years. He has some hope that we will ask him to replace our roof. He phones regularly throughout the year, every two or three months. One year he phoned on New Year's Eve.

"Hello," he said in the slight eastern European accent we'd become accustomed to. "George, here. Would you be thinking of replacing your roof in the coming year?"

It was 10:30 in the evening. The video had just ended, and we were hanging around the kitchen counting down the minutes to midnight. We'd watched the kettle boil and were sharing a teabag: two cups, one bag. I'd brought out the festive tin of left-over Christmas cookies.

"Not right now," my husband told George. "I'm sorry, but we do not need a new roof."

We're pleasant to George because George is pleasant to us, even if he is persistent. "Did he say 'Happy New Year'?" I asked, somewhat anxiously. It was a lonely New Year's Eve: the two of us, the video, the teabag.

"No," my husband said. "Just that he'd call again in three months. Mark that on the calendar. I'm sure George has. It's something we can all look forward to."

Once George left a message on our answering machine asking us to return his call. Which we did thinking for some reason he may be ill and that we were the only people he could contact in his time of need. We were disappointed to reach *his* answering machine. The message said, "Hello. George here. Would you be thinking of replacing your roof in the coming year?"

The way we discovered that George was a Christian happened during a call in which my husband, as usual, had turned him down. Then George tried a new tactic, suggesting we call *him* when we'd decided to proceed with a new roof. "But don't call on a Tuesday evening," he told us. "That's Bible study night."

The fact that George was a Christian interested us; we wondered how far his faith in one day replacing our roof would carry him. And because we're not Christians *per se*, trying as we do to dwell contentedly in transience, we wondered what effect his faith might have on us over time. Would he be calling for the next twenty years? Would the three of us grow old together while our roof overgrew with moss and continued to lose shingles in windstorms, while we continued to gently tell him, "No, thank you, George. Not this year." Would the presence of George in our lives become as comforting as ritual? Would his phone calls become, in spite of our secular orientation, like a knot in the thick rope of our reason that was hauling us through the years?

The idea of our contacting him about the roof was short-lived. Before long his quiet, intermittent calls resumed. What is it, we asked each other that causes George to believe so surely that one day he will replace our roof? And how did we acquire this random person in our lives so that now his calls have become like calls from long-ago friends, both dreaded and strangely desired?

Then after six years this thought occurred and it startled us: The true reason that George is phoning about our roof is that this is his job in life—he is a roofer—and to get jobs he calls people up. He doesn't have a personal relationship with us at all, nor is he calling to facilitate our meditations on the nature of our lives, or even to imbue us with Christian beliefs.

When we thought this thought we felt bad. Bad for having so blithely and self-centredly missed the obvious. Bad that for six years we may have strung along an honest, hard-working man. A decent person. We felt especially mean to have done this. Further, we felt that such meanness of spirit may have contributed to our succession of lonely New Year's Eves, and to our transient existence being, we had to admit, a state less than fulsome.

So we finally asked George to do something about our roof. After six years my husband called him up—it was a Saturday morning—and said, "Now is the time, George."

George didn't sound surprised or overjoyed to hear from us. He merely stated in his usual calm way that he'd arrive at our house that afternoon between the hours of two and four.

When at last we saw him we felt cheered by his appearance; he was exactly as we'd imagined after six years of telephone calls: small, meek, fair-skinned, about sixty-five years old, wearing beige work clothes and a baseball cap. His truck was new and very clean, as we knew it would be.

He nodded to us as he climbed his aluminum ladder to the roof to look things over. From the driveway below we watched him poking at the shingles, and then take a few moments to gaze at the view. A while later we could hear him whistling "Rock of Ages."

When we asked him how he was getting on he called down, shaking his head sadly. "You'll need a complete roof replacement." He was standing on our roof in quiet triumph and telling us, "It's the moss on the shingles. It's the terrible rot within."

And then we couldn't agree more. For the first time in six years we felt as if a load was about to be lifted. The terrible rot within was about to be removed. It was a bright day in early December with the sun glinting off George's glasses as he began his solemn descent down the ladder. Right there in the driveway, as George drove away with the promise of a new roof before Christmas, we began planning a crowded New Year's Eve party—loud, boozy, sinful.

The Breakdown So Far

ON THE SUBJECT OF LITERATURE

1.

Wondered if the vision was worthwhile or if it was dumb; a gully; an antique. Wondered if there was too much feeling about everything, too much seeing of the world's despair. Was overfull with thinking about the tragicomic; the impotence to help or change; the indulgence of seeking perfectly executed moments of attention and regard; the dabbling in nuclear thought, the fabulously impossible, the impossibly rubbishy, the next uncertainty, the next fresh wind. Wondered about the necessity of gratification tricks, the increased wattage of personal pleasure to maintain, if not blindness, then the covert, sidelong view. Could not shut up for wondering.

2.

Referred to our former quirky nurses, the surrealists, the cubists, the beats; observed them acting like volunteer workers for the blind; suggesting the story; the validity of the inspired haul; suffering, and all the rest; tigers, even; the slow shining of expanded connections; the particular voice—thunder! And the absurd; strangeness; the laughter at our scary salesmanship, our arbitrary watchwords— silence; visuals; the scientific method; words; exile; your brother in Disneyland; cunning; song. Remembered: it's a long walk to find a new mind. Remembered: "No new line without a new mind."

3.

Wondered if it is tragicomic that the times we are having now appear on TV in rapid collage, sometimes animated; that our authenticity, as a result, is frequently robbed; that the speed of duplication between what we are and how we are presented further erases reflection, distance, and history; that we are forever here in the lukewarm soup; that there is a living paradise but it's looking dour; that Blake is standing at a low window mourning, not the craft, but the content; that Lorca is fondling his rosary of deaths like an obsessive-compulsive; that irony is eroding fast, like sandstone; that the Dadaists continue to go mad; that, both fearing and yearning for anonymity, many now abandon their art with a grunt.

4.

Assembled the mental health equipment: arrested hopelessness; understood the short rules of meditation and deconstruction; kept skepticism intact; removed self-indulgence; maintained connection to the universe; maintained manoeuvrability; stood witness. Understood the risks: reducing experience to a focus, a narrative arc, the solipsistic, the short light story; suspending thoughts and minds; sweeping aside the large, the inanimate world; regarding dreams as unworthy; exalting over never-lived-in days; nominating oneself for results, for masterpieces; allowing the quest for celebrity to overtake and becoming lost, eaten; keeping Buddha like some high-end perceptual pet.

5.

Admired Norman Levine and Peter Handke, wandering about on trains, and in cities, looking out windows; noting details; the outside world revealed precisely—small events closely observed: snow melting; a parade of hats at a train station; a butterfly's wobble; glow worms; a red-tailed hawk flying across a field of snow. Working at their desks in some high room, alone in winter; draughts through the window frame; a storm brewing, sheet lightning. A kind of exaltation prose, but precise, not hysterical like hunger; prose that tends the fire and the shop; about the fascination with things; in living errant; in randomness and beautiful days; the distinctive now, including moments of sourness; imagination; record keeping; great dread; wild laughs, trembling sweeps; the eye trained for memory; understanding the face of horror but letting the saint be large. Remembered that Chekhov is behind this notion.

6.

Described the irrelevant. Trained the humour. Removed blinkers. Kept the furnishings spare. Feared history. Shunned electronic truths. Shunned money. Remembered that the history of love has resulted in one melody. Traipsed after some Chinese man's sayings, some Indian's, some woman's. Traipsed after an audience. Celebrated both the nightmare and the delight. Trapped experience with words. Exploded, on occasion, with pandemonium. Attempted to melt self-consciousness. Canvassed door to door with song. Scythed moribund visions. Memorized the times. Specified edginess. Maintained aspects of the idiot, the faithful brain. Caught the train. Missed the train. Was found guilty. Was found innocent.

7.

Considered the ideas we funnel into art: the sexual ones; the lives of resurgence; absence; playfulness; merriment; weird fantasy; fakes; fresh views merrily running; making reckless irony enlightenment, a spectacle of encounter; making it very shiny; filling it with heart; spending the world; making melodies of essential truths; creating symphonies, Czeslaws of wonder, everyone with a measure of delight, everyone capable of levitation; remembering former artists and the singular stroke, O'Keefe, for one, and the sublimity of her vision; remembering the lovely black recourse of Burroughs and the days spent in cafés bemoaning the brass consciousness of others; remembering Nabokov's grim monster of common sense and how it must be shot dead; constructing a mental aerobics with stories that include love and the slap of explanation; that include nerve, unadorned; finding what excites, finally, like something pure ...

The Compassionate Side of Nature

For five weeks we watched the video feed of the eagle's nest. A man had placed a video camera in the nest and we along with several million people sat transfixed before computer screens and watched as a nesting pair took turns sitting on two eggs. It was exciting. Soon we would witness the birth. But mysteriously one of the eggs disappeared. It was explained via the newspaper and TV coverage that this often happens with eagles—an egg may be empty. We consoled ourselves: this was raw nature, after all. Then holes were seen in the second egg and we became excited once again—a chick was about to peck its way out of the egg. But it soon became evident that this egg was also empty. There was great sadness among the several million people. But we continued watching to see what might happen next, if anything, and were not disappointed. Three days after the second egg was discarded a new form appeared in the nest—a miniature dachshund wearing a rhinestone collar. We think—and hope—that the dog is a replacement for the failed eggs. You hear about these things, about the compassionate side of nature. For example, mother ducks adopting abandoned kittens, and so on. Perhaps it is the same situation here. The parent eagles at present seem attentive to the dog; they feed it and have in no way harmed it. And they appear mesmerized by the rhinestone collar, staring at it for minutes on end then tapping at it to see what it might be. During sunrise the collar glints spectacularly. But we fear for the dog. What will happen when the eagles decide it's time for it to fly? Will they push it from the nest to its certain death? A rescue operation has been mounted. The world watches as firefighters, who have a well-deserved reputation for rescuing cats from trees, confer with wildlife experts. The great worry is that the eagles will be spooked by human intervention and fly off with the dachshund in a bid to protect it from predators. The dog's name is Bismarck. His owners, an elderly couple who live in a cottage nearby, are receiving trauma counselling. Meanwhile scores of grief workers are on standby should the story end badly.

BUDGIE SUICIDE

We don't know why he did it. He must have been unhappy. It can't have been easy for him—pecking at the bell, hanging about on the pole, staring at the free birds outside the window, the robins, the gulls. Then every night the cage covered with a smelly dish towel. We wonder now if he'd been lonely for his own kind. Maybe he was pining for some squawky budgie sex. We wonder, too, at the strangeness of caging small birds. Like imprisoned souls, my mother-in-law once said.

Day after day we'd watch the budgie hopping along the pole, cocking his head at our huge cratered faces pressed against the cage. Cheep, cheep, cheep, we'd sing, and then scream happily when he paused, seemingly in communication.

We found him hanging from the bell. He had somehow wrapped the bell cord around his neck.

We wonder if our monstrous singing drove him mad.

FUNERAL

We held a funeral for the budgie. I wrapped it in a handkerchief then dug a hole between the marigolds at the side of the house. My husband had said, Flush it down the toilet. It's dead. Get rid of it. But I wanted a proper funeral. I thought I might experience something grand.

I placed the handkerchief in the hole then covered it over. It was a cold afternoon, light rain. Hundreds of birds were perched in the fir trees that border our yard—crows, gulls and smaller chirping birds. We stared at the mound. No one knew what to say. Finally I said, Poor Harry, and the children and I sobbed. When my husband pulled out his imaginary violin and started to play, the birds sent up a terrific screech, flapping their wings, causing the trees to tremble. A budgie requiem, thunderous, there in the rain.

At last, something grand.

Membership Drive

Two members of the Ponderers Club are put in charge of promotion. Membership has been declining. They hold a press conference to kick off their campaign.

There's a popular misconception that pondering is limited to certain kinds of persons, the woman explains from the podium to the one reporter who shows up. Sad sacks, party poopers, doomsters, depressives. This is just not so. Pondering crosses all demographics. Anyone can ponder!

That's right, says the man. Given half a chance pondering could become your basic Everyman condition.

The reporter asks: What? You mean deep thinking?

You could call it that, says the man. But it's much more. It's about experiencing pits of confusion and dread very deeply, and also boring to the core of everything, analyzing meanings and reasons. Laughter, for example. Or transience. Now there's a killer.

Careful, Stan, says the woman. You don't want to scare people off. What Stan means, she says to the reporter, is that ponderers weigh and think things over. "Everything in Ponderation." That's our motto.

Very good, Gwen, says Stan. But what I was trying to say is that ponderers are anti-surface.

No need to get huffy, Stan, I was only …

Then please …

What we're trying to get across here, Gwen says to the reporter, is that there's more to pondering than meets the eye. Pondering can be a fun activity.

Putting a bit of a light spin on things, Stan says. Aren't you Gwen?

The reporter interrupts: But deep thinking. I can't see it. In my pocket of actuality there's the man seeking revenge and the wounded man lying in a hospital bed, and there is constant gunfire but no resolution. What of this?

We live in ponderous times, says Stan.

Okay, but what of the damaged?

Ah, the damaged, says Gwen. This is a music we ponderers know. Also traffic, the tarot, our sacred streets, men in white crying for salvation, clouds. What else?

Ponderence, Gwen, says Stan. We know about ponderance. Which is our mission statement here.

What Stan means, says Gwen, is that we need to keep things on track.

Finally, says Stan.

But deep thinking, says the reporter. I once knew a guy had his head up his ass. All the time. You mean like that? Doesn't seem like a fun thing to me.

Well, said Stan, we'd have to look at what fun really is …

Careful, Stan. There's a preponderance of guys not ready to be outed.

My point exactly, Gwen. Which is why we've got to keep things general. Think of Martin and Gary and Brad and Imelda. They may be extreme ponderers but they deserve our respect like anyone else.

Are you suggesting I don't respect extreme ponderers? Says Gwen.

I'm not suggesting anything, says Stan. I do wish you'd shut up.

Another guy, says the reporter, kept his nose in his armpit. Eventually his brains leaked onto to the floor. I don't call that a fun thing either.

Of all the nerve, says Gwen.

Jesus Loves Me But He Can't Stand You*

I'm drinking alone this Christmas.

I've hired a wino to decorate my home.

I've put a bar in the back of my car so I can drive myself to drink.

Jesus, will you be drinking with me this Christmas?

Will you be thinking of me if you do?

My head hurts and my feet stink.

I don't know whether to kill myself or go bowling.

* Compiled from C&W song titles.

Because of Russell Edson

They are clearing out old theories, their no-longer-fruitful theories: the theory of possible; the theory of want; the theory of restlessness; the theory of wandering; the theory of lizards; the theory of coffee mugs; the theory of figure skating lessons; the theory of clocks.

They've shoved the old theories into garbage bags and set the bags at the end of the driveway. A propped sign says: *Free.*

Behind the living room curtain they watch who stops by.

A boy on a bike takes the theory of lizards.

Predictable, says the son.

A woman with a dog drags off the theory of clocks.

She's old, says the mother.

A woman pushing a stroller grabs the theory of want.

Makes sense, says the father.

The daughter lets out a scream. You threw out the theory of want? While I was still using it?

We thought, says the father.

How could you? It goes with the theory of desire!

We got rid of desire last summer, says the father.

You what? screams the daughter.

Oh dear, says the mother.

We've still got the theory of open, says the son.

Open? shouts the daughter. That old thing? I wouldn't be caught dead.

Dead? says the father. We threw out dead when you were born.

Oh dear, says the mother.

Now I'll never, cries the daughter.

Never? says the father.

Shut up! screams the daughter.

Didn't we give never to your cousin Shirley? says the mother.

Shut up! Shut up!

Sixty Degrees

The first thing our friend talked about was vampires. He was staying overnight at our house and, while we were having tea, he said there was a woman vampire who lived in his building; she was a regular user of the building's swimming pool. This was in Toronto. He knew she was a vampire because she'd told him so. He believed her. Something about her eyes, the way she stared at him while he swam. Apparently she's from Transylvania, he said, which was a dead giveaway. Ha, ha, he said, dead giveaway. Further, this woman was ugly-looking, with dried, yellowed skin like parchment, and stiff, black hair. Not necessarily vampire-describing qualities, he admitted, and said he only mentioned her looks because they contributed to the menace she exuded. She was about forty-five years old. He, on the other hand, was several years older, a celebrated poet and an artist, a man we admired because he lived, we believed, in a permanent state of wonder. He told us that the vampire followed him into the building's sauna, sat close to him, and pinched his knee. He said he'd never been accosted by a vampire before, and that the incident had scared him. *Freaked* him, was the word he used. He ran from the sauna. This happened during the day and we asked why a vampire was on the loose during the day; we thought they did their evil work at night. Special powers, he said, maybe it's different for the women ones, and maybe they have different rules. A few days later, while he swam lengths—again in the daytime—he told us the vampire swam across the pool and slammed into the side of his body. On purpose, leaving a bruise. This vampire assault was the reason, he believed, that his left eye had later gone funny and filled up with blood. Soon after, the vampire disappeared, left the building. Gone on a trip, he supposed, back to Transylvania. The doctor said his eye problem was curious and ordered tests. Meanwhile he'd formed a swimming pool committee. This had to do with the temperature of the swimming pool water, and was not exclusively about the vampire, although she had been involved. There were some residents who liked the water warm, he told us, and some who liked the water cold. The cold water lovers, he said, were dominating the pool temperature. A quiet battle had ensued, which included the bribery of the building manager for access to the pool's thermostat. The cold water lovers, he said, were more affluent than the warm water lovers; they could afford the bribery fees. Because of this they were winning the war. The warm water lovers were mainly a group of frail pensioners, students, and people handicapped in some way, like him with the vampire bruise and the bloody eye, and, as usual, this group was being marginalized and trod upon by those with money. Sixty degrees. That was the temperature they were battling over. The cold water lovers preferred sixty degrees; the warm water lovers, seventy to eighty. Naturally, he said, the woman vampire, when she was in residence, had been among the cold water lovers, no doubt campaigning for an even colder temperature than sixty degrees. Somewhere around freezing, he imagined. Meanwhile, he was waiting for the test results about his injured eye. It was no longer filled with blood but it was sore, and his vision had become impaired. When he left for the West Coast there had been no resolution about the water temperature, nor had he received the test results. But he was glad to leave the vampire behind. At least he thought he'd left the vampire behind. Did we think he had? Yes, we did. Did we think she might find out where he was now living and follow him to the coast? No, we didn't think she would. That's good, he said, she's probably on a vampire vacation; it's spring in Transylvania; she's sure to stay there for the summer. Or maybe she's attending a vampire convention, or a vampire reunion. Or, ha, ha, he said, a vampire festival where hundreds of vampires gather to have workshops and panels and suck each other's blood and talk with agents about selling the film rights to their books. He then mentioned the movie versions about vampires that he loved, the old black and white ones made in the forties and fifties, especially *Son of Dracula*. He liked the Bram Stoker versions, too, and the new movie just out, *Van Helsing*, which, he said, was doing well at the box office. He checked the movie grosses on his computer every night, he said, the daily takes for all the movies playing in theatres across North America, and in the rest of the world. He didn't ask to use our computer that night, though; he only asked for something to eat because he'd missed dinner on the ferry ride over. We gave him a late meal of chickpea soup left over from our dinner, and toast and cheese, and a plate of sweet mixed pickles. He'd missed dinner, he explained, because on the ferry he'd been sitting beside an old woman who had a walker parked in front of her, and they'd struck up a conversation. The old woman was worried about how she was going to get off the ferry when it docked. Where was the exit for foot passengers? He said he'd find out for her because he too was a foot passenger and this was important information. The ferry employee told him: See that wall? The one close to where you're sitting? Well, when the ferry docks, a door opens in that wall, and then you walk through it. He reported back to the old woman: when the ferry docks, you walk through that wall; the wall becomes a door. The old woman became agitated. I'm not walking through any wall, she told him. I'll help you, he offered. No thank you, she said, I'll wait here until my family comes and gets me. When the ferry docked he said it was like magic. Suddenly a door appeared in the wall, and everyone walked through it. The old woman stayed seated and refused to move. When he left her, two ferry employees were trying to convince her to walk through the wall but she wouldn't budge. He, on the other hand, was not afraid. He walked through the wall with the other passengers, down the steel mesh ramp that showed sea water sparkling far below, and reached the waiting room at the terminal. It was wonderful, he said, walking along with the disembarking passengers. Like being safe in the middle of a herd of humans where no marauding predator could pick you off. Wouldn't it be wonderful, he asked, to be all the time moving through your life like that? It made him think of *National Geographic* specials on TV, the shows about herds of running gazelles and stalking lions. Only the straying young or the infirm were slaughtered. It made him think, once again, about the woman vampire. You don't think she's singled me out for some reason do you? You don't think she'll bother me again? I'm not very gazelle-like. No, we said, it's likely she's someone who thinks she's a vampire but is actually a disturbed person with many problems of her own. Oh, he said, that's a relief. Are you sure? Yes, we said, absolutely. We didn't know if he believed us; though we were certain that an excellent poem or painting would result from his experience.

POOF

A doctor tells a woman during her regular checkup that her black hole is getting larger. Each of us possesses a black hole, he says, because each of us resides in a separate universe. Eventually we disappear down our own black holes. Then, poof, we're gone! It's neat. It's tidy. It's basic science.

The woman does not share the doctor's delight. We are one universe, one brain, she says. We are a flock of humans. And I won't be disappearing, I'll be recycled. I'll be taking my place in the eternal white light. Thereafter to become who knows what? A worm, perhaps. A swan. Trust a male to come up with a black hole. That worn out womb thing. That vagina-gobbling-you-up thing. Crawl back in a hole if you want to. Not me. I'm spring-boarding in a different direction.

Have it your way, says the doctor. But it's a proven fact. As we age our black holes get larger. The universe is all about black holes.

Gobble, gobble, gobble, says the woman.

Just then a great black thing and a great white thing collide in the doctor's office and an even greater grey thing is born. It looks like a cloud of ashes.

My god! The doctor and the woman cry as they immediately age, wither, die and disappear.

Imagine their surprise …

A LITTLE SOMETHING

Fifty thousand vaginas were sent through the mail. Free samples. Part of an ad campaign for a revived play. We couldn't get ours open. It was shut tighter than a bivalve. "Useless!" My husband cried. "You call that a talking vagina?" I knew how he felt. Last week, a shriveled penis was left on the doorstep. Another free sample. It came with a card: "A little something from the Goddess." Goddess is a line of lubricants. The penis was supposed to enlarge and chase you around the house and call you baby when rubbed with the cream. No dice. I couldn't even get it to squeak. The cream's a fraud. The penis lay on the dining room table like an old carrot. Then the cat dragged it off but gave up trying to chew it because the skin was so tough.

We've buried the vagina and the penis together in the back garden. Perhaps a little something might erupt through the dirt this spring.

SPRING IN NORTH AMERICA

A man sits on a city curb with fir seedlings attached to his hair and a sign that reads: *The Civil War Starts Here.*

A girl called Plain Trouble sits nearby. Her sign reads: *Potent Guys Please Apply.* She wants a baby but most of the sperm is dead.

A boy holding a plastic cup for change joins them. His name is Ozone. His sign reads: *I've Got Early Decadence Syndrome.*

A gang of children passes by and throws hamburger cartons at them. Otherwise—anonymity.

It is spring in North America. The sun shines in biblical slants through the buildings. Light glints off windows, chrome, sunglasses ...

A crew across the street has set up a sign that says, *Filming in Progress.* They're working on a popular TV show called *Final Decisions.* Today's segment follows a woman while she purchases a dress for an important End Times Banquet. To spice things up the producers will add a vicious white monkey who is infected with the Ebola virus. After the dress is purchased the monkey will chase the woman through city streets.

A crowd gathers to watch the shoot. Many hold placards with the shopping woman's name writ in large letters. Beneath her name: *We Love You.*

A derelict couple pauses beside the three on the curb. They're worn out from wandering and sit down. The woman carries a sign that reads: *Who Would Have Dreamed?* The man: *Poems by Bob Buddhism.*

Since it is spring in North America, there's warmth on faces, hands; a gentle breeze blowing cartons along the pavement …

FRIDGE MAGNET PEOPLE

On the plane to Toronto I sat beside a man who was touring cross-country with fridge magnets. "I've got the latest thing in fridge magnets," he said, snapping open his case. "They're called 'Types.'" He showed me his samples—miniature people that lit up when stuck to a smooth surface. There was a woman jogger in a blue track suit; a bank manager with a menacing look on his face holding a sheaf of documents; a kid in a backwards ball cap balanced on a skateboard; an old woman in a fur coat with a look of pride on her face. The salesman was doing five home shows in two weeks.

I started seeing fridge magnet people everywhere. For example—myself. I was a woman in black clutching a book, the latest thing in imagination this season. I was on a book tour—one city in half a day. I lit up when stuck to a podium.

The stewardess lit up when her hands made contact with the tray while serving our drinks. She told us she was going on tour next week with a cookbook for people with gluten intolerance. There'd be TV interviews throughout the province of Ontario.

In the hotel café the waitress lit up while cleaning the counter and telling me about her sulphur-crested cockatoos. She'd be touring with them in summer—four bird shows in three weeks.

When I returned home my husband—middle-aged, jeans, grey beard—lit up when his hand slapped his forehead; he'd had a brain wave. "Why haven't I thought of this before?" he said. "Smith!" nodding at our nineteen-year-old cat. "I'm organizing a motivational tour. Smith's story can provide inspiration to elderly cats and their owners." The cat lit up when stuck to my husband's lap.

At the Dollar Store the gum-chewing teenager with the eyebrow ring lit up while working the shiny keys of the cash register. She told me she was going on tour with her Dad. "He's filming the faceless," she said. "There aren't that many faceless people left. He's found one old guy hiding out in a shed in Saskatchewan. It's that guy's boring story. Boring's the new cool."

Alighting on smooth surfaces—it seemed some kind of key ...

Perpetual Coda

1.

We bring our perfect intelligence to bear upon the situation, which is to say, our lives, which is to say our reasons; where the essential story is the one in which the world outlives our dreams, where human death outlives our knowing; where the sorry view is the one in which we stand, step, weep, and die; where bitterness produces stories that caricature mankind, hence our need for love, that neutralizing force we wear on our sleeves like an IV drip of soda; where memory is the salvation of the retired and the overwhelmed, but frequently a gift we give ourselves; where most understandings are accidental, the result of an ontological crapshoot; where self-admiration is a violent knowing that obscures all light; where the mythical forest is ourselves; where we lunch on lyric expressions, imagining rescue, escape; where our time demands simplicity as counterpoint to excessive detail—or so it seems—like a basic formula; where I am a woman stumbling without hope towards enlightenment as surely as if it were heaven; where I am a woman whose steps are dogged by violent reasons.

2.

We bring our perfect intelligence to bear upon small-time meta-physical points; where hope propels us towards heartbreaking wisdoms; where any church attempts to neutralize the natural acids that would caricature mankind; where love is our reward delivered often without enlightenment as though through a fog; where we lunch on various Buddhas still imagining rescue, escape; where hope is pinned on eternity; where thinking demands simplicity as counterpoint to excessive heart; where I am a woman participating in the small-time greedy view; where I am a woman stumbling towards love, light and the mythical forest.

3.

We bring our hunger to bear upon the situation, which is to say, our reasons; where the story, like a basic dream, is the one in which we stand, step, weep, and die; where understanding is frequently accidental, or the result of formula; where some of us engage in the work of archiving metaphors; where some of us can name at least seven bitter stories that caricature mankind; where love is the story of our heartbreaking wisdoms; where memory is the story of our IV drip of routine, which is to say, our violent knowing; where in every human death there is a story about land mines; where I am a woman stumbling towards the perpetual coda; where I am a woman stumbling as though through a fog.

Breakdown of the Month Calendar

January. Outside, the everlasting wheezes and falters. The dog poses on the community picnic table then vanishes. The town is flabby and grey. At home there is a tight limit on table language.

February. Mother's mind goes missing on a drive for soft ice-cream. A return to the picnic table turns up a bird's skull. Grandma wears work boots and lime-green stretch pants to Grandpa's funeral. The language on the fridge magnet says *You Are Loved.*

March. At home Mother's mind is found buried beneath the laundry. Sister writes a poem in praise of emotion. A new dog is bought and named Odysseus. Outside, the everlasting is crackling and green.

April. It rains on the town for thirty straight days. For thirty days Brother watches TV. Father unplugs the sink, the toilet and the storm drains. Mother's mind scurries off in a torrent of ditch water.

May. Brother gets a prize for taking a bath. Grandma wears a black sarong and bare feet to Old Age Bingo. Sister writes a hymn about dread. The planet tilts nearer the sun.

June. Outside, the everlasting bubbles and bursts. Mother's mind returns inside a yellow helium balloon. The balloon settles in a back-yard tree and glows at night like a lamp. Father lies on the living room rug laughing hysterically.

July. Odysseus begins his wanderings through the blue and silver town. The balloon bursts when a robin lands on its surface. Grandma breaks her arm climbing the tree to gather pieces of Mother's mind. The robin is taken to the vet.

August. The car breaks down on a trip for Krazy Glue. For two weeks, the glue keeps Mother's mind attached to her brain. One evening the everlasting, the town and Mother's mind are cast in a lovely bronze light. The car breaks down on a trip for pizza.

September. Brother wins a prize for taking out the garbage. Mother gets a new broom to commemorate renewed effort. Grandma gets a new pot to bang on because she's not dead yet. Brother wins new love—the vet's comely assistant.

October. Mother's mind hitches a ride on her broom and soars towards the moon. Father says the trick in life is to keep your eyes averted. Grandma says the treat is hardly worth the effort. Grandma runs off with the bingo caller.

November. Outside, the everlasting is ragged and brown. Odysseus returns with Mother's mind on a leash. Father lies on the kitchen floor laughing and laughing. The planet tilts away from the sun.

December. Sister writes a poem about renewal. Brother wins a prize for leaving home. Mother's mind is housed with the budgie. The car breaks down on a trip for birdseed.

BAD BOY

My husband hides lethal chemicals the way some men hide pornography, guns or a bad drinking problem. When I discovered a sealed box of Diazinon lodged inside the toilet tank, I became suspicious and asked him about it. "Guilty," he said, and went on to tell me about his club, which is called Chemical Men. He said he hoped I'd understand.

He's belonged to the club for eleven years. It's a secret club, which is always the best kind, my husband says, a club dedicated to the preservation of antique chemicals. Members collect DDT, napalm and unopened cans of Raid from the middle part of the last century, and then they trade these items, or sell them. They have a monthly Internet newsletter and, each autumn, an underground festival which is virtual but well attended. According to my husband, members of the club are especially interested in the uses of industrial chemicals for the home garden.

This past week my husband says he'd been involved in an Internet bidding war over a vial of Agent Orange. It's been exciting for him, he says, and is relieved, now, to be able to share this excitement with me. So far he hasn't had a definite buy, but he's hopeful. Apparently, collecting lethal chemicals has become a hobby for him; much like the hobby his father had which was collecting silver foil from cigarette packages. His father, who'd spent his working life as a travelling salesman for Bic pens, rolled the foil into balls the size of basketballs. No one is sure why he did this, other than for the calm it gave him. When he died, five silver balls were bequeathed to my husband, representing an adult life of smoking, collecting foil and single-minded rolling. Curiously my father-in-law did not die of lung cancer, but of old age.

My husband is quick to point out that besides the benefits of engaging in a hobby—old age not withstanding—collecting lethal chemicals is important archival work. Like his father, he looks upon his collection as something to leave the kids. "In fifty years time, do you know what these babies will be worth?" he asks, referring to his stockpile, now covering a quarter of the garage floor after retrieval from the several hiding places around the house and yard—inside the old croquet bag; above the ceiling tiles in our son's former bedroom; behind the hot water tank in the laundry room; within a specially designed space in the wood pile.

My husband is gleeful telling me this, but I suspect that his glee has more to do with hoodwinking me for eleven years than in leaving a legacy for the kids. Eleven years ago I declared our property a chemical-free zone. All herbicides and pesticides were banned. "Here is a corner of the world that will remain free of contamination," I said. I was proud of my stand and told our neighbors, the retired psychiatrist and his wife. Now I'm remembering how they were taken aback with the news but quickly recovered to register blank agreement. I'm also remembering how over the years I've seen them— usually at dusk—creeping between their rows of tomato plants wearing face masks and carrying buckets and spray nozzles. For some reason I didn't associate this behavior with the use of lethal chemicals; I'd assumed they were using something safe, like soap suds. It's obvious now what they were doing, heedless of soil contamination in their quest for massive tomatoes. My husband has now confirmed that they are also members of Chemical Men.

I am convinced that my husband has been dipping into his collection. The slugs in the garden did not pack up and move of their own volition. I realize this now. Before then our yard was a maze of weeds, grasses, wild flowers and rangy, creeping roses instead of the monster-size flowers we have now. By all accounts, they should be bug-eaten and straggly. I thought these vibrant over-bloomers grew without much effort other than admiring them and pulling the odd weed. I thought they had achieved balance with the natural world and that they were, in fact, thriving in a happy, chemical-free way. Obviously, I was wrong.

Still, I have to acknowledge my husband's ability to carry off his eleven-year practical joke. The thrill he had while hoodwinking me must have been enormous, not to mention the secret fun he's had when I gushed over the wisteria blooms, or the creeping veronica, or the profusion of tulips, and so forth. No doubt the psychiatrist and his wife were in on the joke.

Registering my dismay, my husband claims that he used the chemicals because of me; that it was an act of love because I enjoy continual bloom in a plant and am saddest in winter when there is only holly and snowberry to look at. But there is nothing sadder than a man armed with a canister of herbicide and a battery-powered light strapped to his head while sneaking about the yard at midnight, and I am not even slightly convinced. My husband is not a violent man but I think the thrill he gets from handling the destruction that resides in lethal chemicals must be overwhelming. This thrill, coupled with the thrill of hoodwinking me, further produces in him a feeling of euphoria; he's being a bad boy when he does this. I think at heart that this is what my husband is—a bad boy who has got away with things.

Fortunately, I am a good girl. And I am reasonable. I have given him twenty-four hours to begin the detoxification process that will return our yard to its essential condition of weeds and dead things. I am not saying, *or else*. I am not saying I will pack my bags and become my own hobby tomato. I am saying, "Just because some of us can read and write and do a little math, that doesn't mean we deserve to conquer the Universe."

THE NORTH POLE
2009

The North Pole

We're keeping Daddy company. He's been under the quilt for two hundred and thirty-seven days.

On the living room couch. It's some kind of record.

No, he's not sick. Not in the usual way.

The remote's in his right hand. You can't see it. It's under the quilt. His hand gets cold.

Quit it, Dustin. No one wants to see the remote.

That's nearly eight months of non-stop TV.

Quit it, I said. Find something to do.

Seven. The kid's seven. We had him late.

He's on the couch all the time. Except to use the bathroom. Eats and sleeps on the couch. The TV going night and day.

I watch from the recliner. Stig's on the hard-backed chair. Stig's our boarder. We watch it with him.

Pretty much all the time.

A trio travels to Transylvania to destroy a werewolf queen.

One of the late-night movies we've seen. Stig keeps track.

ETS. Daddy's got ETS.

End Time Syndrome.

He turned forty-four last July.

Well, it starts out gradual. Sneaks up on you.

All the bad news. You get shell-shocked. Lose meaning. Feel helpless. There are so many things.

Whew.

Dying trees. Everyone getting cancer, especially little kids.

No, not you, Dustin.

Hurricanes. The planet heating up. Pandemics. A new one every year. Poisoned chocolates from China. Animals dying off. You name it.

People shut down. Become a former.

What they were before they got ETS.

Daddy? A baggage handler at the airport.

Hairy creatures from earth's core latch onto human necks.

At least he's not totally gone. Like some. At least he's got his cause.

Saving the North Pole.

Leave Daddy's quilt alone.

Kid never sits still. The meds don't help.

That's what I said. The North Pole. Melting ice.

Sorry, ice melt. Glacier melt.

He gets mad if I say it wrong.

Gets squirmy.

He's staying on the couch until the ice stops melting.

That's what he said eight months ago. Before he stopped talking.

He's serious. Won't have ice cubes in his pop. Nothing from the freezer. Nothing that melts.

Well, what can you do?

Just keep him comfortable, that's all. And he's got his sign. He likes his sign. It's over there by the couch.

Hold up your sign. Hold up your sign.

Sometimes he'll hold up his sign. His protest sign: Save The North Pole. Sometimes he'll wave his sign at the TV.

Your guess is as good as mine. But we respect his reasons. Whenever he feels like waving it, I guess.

That's right, Dustin, Santa Claus lives at the North Pole. And polar bears. And fluffy arctic cotton grass.

We're home-schooling him.

If all the ice melts we'll drown. That's a fact.

All of us, Dustin.

A while back I contacted the *Guinness Book of Records*.

They weren't interested. They said lots of people watch TV forever. But how many do it for a cause?

Astrology influences the prowess of a third-rate boxer.

That was a good one.

A ravenous snake terrorizes hapless Koreans.

Also good.

A hologram sings for a struggling band.

Thank you, Stig.

Stig's Mom's got it. She's in the psych ward. A former real estate agent. National sales leader for 2006.

Three spirits try to restore a woman's faith in true love.

Stig again.

He was in my group. My ETS support group. Needed a place to live.

We get disability. Plus money for Stig. Foster care money.

I've stopped going.

To my group. What's the use?

Stig? Seventeen. The black cape is recent. So is the white paint on his face and hands.

Rural Vermonters try to bury a corpse, more than once.

I hope Stig's not getting it.

Pretty soon there'll be more of them than us. Ha, ha. Who's the zombie?

I know. It's not funny. That's another ETS symptom. Nothing's funny.

News. Sitcoms. Cartoons. Talk shows. It's all the same to Daddy. He doesn't care what he watches.

Neither do I for that matter.

Stig likes the late-night movies. That's all he'll talk about. Dustin, well—Dustin.

That's what the social worker said. It's all the candy he eats. Too much sugar.

What's it to you?

We all eat candy.

A carpenter takes control of a Jewish woman's button store.

An art thief steals an insurance investigator's heart.

Napoleon Bonaparte concocts a plan to reclaim his throne.

Don't get Stig going. That's how it starts. One-track obsessions.

Mine's pretending I'm on TV being interviewed about ice. Melting ice.

Sorry. Ice melt.

What?

A former exotic dancer.

I wasn't so heavy then.

Advice Old and New

To ensure that a change in life or in love will be a good one the old advice is to throw hot stones against the door of where you are living. Besides providing you with temporary good luck, this action will cause all liquids in the vicinity to flow more freely. For example, an increase in the milk production of neighbouring cows will occur; rivers will become fast flowing; heavy rain will be unleashed from suddenly ashen skies; your blood will quicken its course through your body causing your face to flush, your muscles to strengthen, and your energy level to soar.

You will need this energy. Because along with good luck comes bad luck, often in the form of malevolent spirits who will tamper with your liquid moments causing your thoughts to become like rooms filled with landmines, causing gleefulness to vanish, dread to be restored.

The new advice says you must do several strenuous things to ensure that bad luck doesn't gain the upper hand, but so far we don't know what these strenuous things might be.

Perhaps there's a list somewhere.

Maybe you can find it.

Or figure one out.

The best I know is to wear yellow and hold your breath.

ARDENT SPIRIT

We created a drink and called it *Ardent Spirit*. It was made of Pepto-Bismol and Aquavit, two parts to one, the water of life tempered with a calming agent for the peptic glands. The drink became popular with old men and women who complained they could no longer forget. For some reason the hoped-for return to childhood had been denied them. Not being able to forget meant dwelling in a bald, unwanted understanding. *Ardent Spirit* combined mercy with repose to counteract this understanding. It did this by hiding the secret caverns in the old people's minds, the places where they slaughtered their dreams. After one glass nothing was remembered of them at all.

It is said that we keep the worst for last. It is also said that in order to endure our predicament we've got to love the truth. But that's like loving your executioner.

The Gnats That Blur Our Vision

We turned off the lights to see through screens into other worlds. To absolutely lose ourselves in madness, passion, abandon, sublimity. To fully fucking wreak shit with our puny conscious minds. Because each of these new worlds has its own physics, its own creator. Because after everything the screens were so lovely, glowing, casting a deeper spell, allowing multiple universes, allowing ecstasy. "Because after something comes nothing. No enemy armada. No music. No score." Just us and our control of the unseen. Plus the satisfying wasteland at the end of rapture. Our only requirement is to have a kick drum knocking at all times, occasionally wind chimes.

Still, the old deities hover nearby like a cloud of gnats. Some burrow beneath our eyelids and blur our vision. This has happened more often than we liked. One such gnat was especially persistent. This was the blind seer Jorge Luis Borges. Suddenly our eyes would feel scratchy, as if a handful of dust had been thrown at them, and then, when we'd try to rub them clean, there he'd be trailing his entourage of former selves, multiples of Borges.

"Every man runs the risk of being the first immortal," he and his younger selves would intone, their hawk-like profiles flickering across our screens.

"Every man runs the risk of disconnecting his subconscious."

We'd fiddle with the controls.

"Every puny ecstasy rushes toward its own demise. Not even a bird's trill can save you."

We'd shrug him off, having no time for the prophesy of dead seers. Having time only to execute our parts as the kings and queens of the graceful glide. For the engine running mankind's ambitious extinction.

Our eyes glow like abalone swans in a pool of glare.

THE ACT IN ETERNITY

There are billions in the cast. We each have a part and our parts keep changing. There is no rehearsal. You get to say your lines only once. Your act moves along quickly, though much of the time you are asleep. Much of the time you are speechless. There is no alternative; you have to join the cast. Most of us are bit players. There is no one director; you direct each other as best you can. Sometimes the lighting is extraordinary: aurora storms, lunar halos, northern lights; sometimes it is precious: the sun on a violet. The intensity varies. Often there is only blackness. Time is an invisible curtain that rises and falls on a whim. The audience is each other. We clap when happy, boo when mad, howl when afraid. There is much apprehension; we are never sure how to act, never understand the motivation for our parts. No one can tell us why. We create prizes to keep up morale, create reason, hope. Poets in their gardens praise beauty; their poems are like Morse Code tapping S.O.S. through the ages. Billions hear this tapping on the way to their graves. At the same time billions more of us are created. Yet the story is always the same. This is something we don't like. We keep on acting as if our lives depend upon it.

Against all odds some of us adhere to a favourite part. I am the strange woman with the deepening walk who carries a two-by-four over one shoulder. You are the large man sitting in the fire; flames all 'round, not feeling the heat.

ANSWERING THE CHILDREN

Q: Where will it end?

A: In the great haul of history.

Mostly there will be history. You must realize this. One foot following another without options. And everywhere there will be graves and because of graves grown people will be gathered together sobbing while children sing and dance nearby. Thus the ages follow one another. This is called the great haul of history.

Q: Where will it end?

A: In bankruptcy.

Understand that you are a registered world with a finite spending capacity. But also that you need not live solely in the required now. In plain English you can step across the sideline, borrow time. This is something we do. Have our eggs in more than one world. In worlds filled with imagination, say, or northern lights, or lucky stars.

Q: Where will it end?

A: We love you.

You can thank your windfall days for that. Now please resume your singing. We don't want to say too much.

THE GOD OF BANALITY

We have washed the house in morning rain. Bathed the children with words plucked from the lips of poets. Bathed ourselves with the music that inhabits the end of dreams, three descending notes of rapturous birdsong.

We have swept the pathway of ashes, tethered our farm animals to oak trees, chopped wood at sunrise, sprinkled salt and milk across our doorsteps, lit outdoor fires for the morning feast where eggs boiled with pig's snouts and magical words have been offered and consumed. We have re-told the death anecdotes and the tales of narrative luck that allow us to take heart in this world.

We do these things every morning to ensure the enduring presence of the god in our lives. The god of the everyday—soothing, predictable, common to all—a singing hologram that lives in dust.

PLAY BUTTON

I want to be the play button that sends out laughing songs. Thereby reprising the merry view. Where its folk reign. Sacred champagne. An endless ticker tape parade.

I'll even project pictures of the world's dumb work. What we do, the mush of things, the clinking animosities, the wondrous starving in the wondrous world.

If I can stay the old form, thoughtful and sweet from the history store.

If I can be a slot machine for Chekhov. A one-armed bandit winning a jackpot of sight. Though I'll settle for a sly aside of knowing why. And how and when. A merry-go-round as to words, tra la ...

THE SECRET PILLARS OF THE UNIVERSE

All men named Bob* are secret pillars of the universe, as are all women named Janice.* We read about it in *National Geographic*— "Scientists Unlock the Secret of the Universe." Graphs, a map, and stunning pictures accompanied the article. We read it with relief. Now that the secret has been revealed we can let go of our worries. There are living people who are responsible for all the physical matter in the universe as well as the entirety of space and time; it doesn't have to be us holding things together. In fact, it *can't* be us since our names are neither Bob nor Janice, but Darcie and Dwayne. All that is required is that we go about our daily business of observing the weather and cooking our oatmeal. That's it. Big Bangs, Standard Models, Big Crunches, Local Bubbles, Black Holes, Negative Energy, Dark Matter, and the End of the Universe needn't concern us. We can relax. The Bobs and Janices are hard at work.

Only they don't know it, don't know that they are secret pillars of the universe and hence are working on our behalf. Their work is un-self-conscious. Blind. Dumb. This is what the scientists discovered: secret pillars don't realize their importance, their *necessity*. If they were ever to attain a full understanding of their life's purpose they would immediately die, go mad, or be replaced. Who or what does the replacing? So far this is unknown, but the fact that they immediately lose their mortal power is the reason the article didn't use their real names. Naming them would be like taking aim and firing.

Like causing the universe to wobble, maybe even to disappear.

* Not their real names.

We assume that the pillars are good and selfless people—quiet, intuitive champions of the beautiful, the true and the just. We are told that their work is much like that of Atlas from Greek mythology who was punished by Zeus for picking the wrong side in the Olympian war. There's a picture of Altas in the article. Naked and blind, he's bent over from carrying the celestial sphere on his shoulders, an unendurable load to be sure but not, the article explained, as weighty as our whole universe.

Researchers have isolated the two genes responsible for causing a person to become a secret pillar. They are the Bob* Gene and the Janice* Gene. This is what they are called though the names are fictitious and in no way reveal the identity of their carriers. The genes were discovered during routine autopsies of the suddenly dead and scientists are now working on developing a blood test which will determine the gene's presence in an individual, work that is not without ethical controversy.

The Bob and the Janice genes become activated either at birth when, unbeknownst to their parents, the name is assigned, or later on if the secret name is used as a diminutive or pet name, or if a person unwittingly changes his or her name either legally or otherwise. This last instance is called a Cosmic Conversion.

There's an infrared picture of what is thought to be a Cosmic Conversion on the third page of the article. It's of a "New Bob," a person aged thirty-two who for some inexplicable reason decided to change his name from Robbo. The special camera, while obscuring his facial features, has caught a shimmering cloud that engulfs the new Bob; it looks like an iridescent soap bubble. Scientists suspect that this soap bubble may be an indication of secret pillardom. "New Bob" in the picture is cradling a pet ferret while behind him lies a trashed Harley Davidson motorcycle and a burning club house. He is a replacement Bob.

* Their real names.

We believe he's Dwayne's nephew, though we have been advised not to pursue this notion because if his true identity were revealed then that would be the end of the "New Bob," the end of a pillar of the universe. We wouldn't want to be responsible, would we?

A purely personal conjecture on the part of me, Darcie Sloan,[*] is that if I, for example, were to possess the Janice gene it would mean that I too, am a secret pillar of the universe. And so might you be, and you, and you. Though scientists advise it's unwise to go snooping after our true selves as their autopsy tables prove. It is better, they tell us, to be content with the micro-universe we know, the one that came into being at our births. Appreciate the spectacular light show that includes all forms of matter and energy and the physical laws and constraints that govern them, they tell us, and leave the heavy work of holding up the universe to the unknowing Bobs and the Janices— and to them.

* Not my real name.

EQUIPMENT FOR THE ENDURANCE OF LOVE

Glee. The choice of a resident choir is important. Gleefullness is influenced by atmosphere, and since appearance is the most important component of atmosphere, it is crucial that your choir be pleasing to the eye as well as to the ear. A capella choirs make the best home choirs and may be made up of angels, birds, or human beings. The choir should be portable and able to perform four-part harmonies, or more, on demand!

Mnemotechny. Again it is the meticulous Germans who explain that the house where a love affair is under siege should be adorned with copper engravings, pointillist paintings and granite carvings of your ancestors. The secret of enduring love, they tell us, is to display these items about your rooms and move them often, but gently. A certain high-class school of thought in France disagrees, dispensing with procedure all together. Their method of constructing mnemotechny is to prohibit deliberateness, insisting that results can best be achieved with the random and often violent pairing of inharmonious elements—the Buddha enshrined in a Barbie castle would be an obvious example. The French method, it should be pointed out, is a professional one, and unless expertly executed may result in the merely droll.

WHAT WE NEED

A handler. A hand up. A hand-hold. A Han(d)sel and Gretel. A handstand. Handlebars. Handball. A handbook. Handwriting. A handicap. A handgun. A hand grenade. Handcuffs. Hands wringing. A handle on it. A hand out. A handmaiden. A handyman. A hand job. A handbag. A hand mirror. A handout.

A good hand. A hand over a fist. A hand over a hand. A handsome thank you.

A hearty handshake. A handful of good luck. The sound of one hand clapping.

A handspring. Another handspring ...

Pulse*

The timeline is shrinking. We are entering the risk zone. Consumers are in the dump, victims of financial advisors, psychopaths, corrupt CEOs, their own greed. We wonder: should we stay in the dump or should we go? Cut our losses or take a wait and see approach? Spend what's left on Christmas or cut back, hunker down? It's a rich mystery. It's feared the crisis could get much worse. Surplus has been scaled back by billions. What does this mean? Falling prices in a broad range of categories have created a nightmare scenario that worries the top cop. He's pledged to end disorder. We're not in the best place on earth any more. This much is clear. This much has been repeatedly stated. The homeless are no longer docile or whacked out but angry. Their numbers have swollen to include former haves. Now everyone's in danger of slipping into the red. It's feared the bloodbath's about to begin. We are in deeply negative territory. We are plunging hard and fast into meltdown. It is feared we are headed beyond what is known.

---

* Compiled from newspaper headlines, late 2008.

THE MENTOR

There isn't a hole he hasn't stood in with measuring tape and clipboard surveying the contours for metaphor and flesh. The holes in our perception and understanding of things; the holes in the blankets we cover ourselves with, hiding out from each other and from life; the holes which are questions, areas of worry and pain and love that we try to find answers to.

For years I peered over the edges of these holes as he worked below, handing him shovels and ropes as required, straining to see the precise measurements he was taking, the notations he made on the clipboard strung around his neck like a postmodern cross. But somehow I was never there when the magic—the pyrotechnic words—appeared. And then I wandered off and discovered that instead of the holes it was the waters that interested me more. Ebb, flow, currents, ferry boat rides ...

This business of creating with words is about not telling lies. You begin and you speak directly. You don't hide behind your words. You get equal billing with them. You're a matched set. It's a combination, but it's not locked. You say what you have to say and you move on. You leave the words, and what they have created. You steer your slow boat beyond them.

To the Author

I was reading your book about the world's natural intricacies, and how landscape consists of the multiple overlapping of forms that exist in a given space in a moment of time.

I thought: So that's what it is! And put the book down and gazed out the window.

The light was yellow and grey; it was mid-afternoon, late fall. There was smoke from burning leaves, a film of cloud, a smudged-looking sun.

I opened the window and leaned on the sill, the better to notice the overlapping forms of the landscape. The air felt cool. Soggy poplar leaves were plastered to the hood of the Toyota; the stand of black bamboo beside the driveway shone from the recent rain. Further off lay a strip of wet asphalt, and beyond that, the sea between firs.

Suddenly the sun broke through, bronzing everything. A moment of time was never so beautiful! This is when, without warning, I experienced surrender. I hadn't planned on that, to move from cataloguing forms—as you suggest in your book—to abandoning time and desire. Your book hadn't prepared me for that.

To Be Continued

Last night we returned to the beach to see the massed gulls. So many were circling the sky overhead as we walked that we were certain we'd find them perched on the rocks as before. There was a strong wind and the sun had broken through the heavily overcast sky so that the underbellies of the gulls were illuminated, flashing white as they rode the wind. But the beach was empty of birds. The herring must have moved farther down the inlet. The strong wind, cold on our faces, pushed at the sea with such force that whitecaps had formed. The light on the small surf, on the overhanging arbutus trees lining the beach, and on the larger firs and cedars beyond them was green and yellow. The scene was hectic, exciting, with the cawing birds overhead. We climbed the rocks and stood looking out, the dog beside us. The wind blew our hair back and the dog's fur was blown flat against her body; she angled her nose and sniffed the windy air. When we returned to the path along the shore we saw uneven lines of grey and brown herring roe spread along the beach. They were woven amongst the seaweed, and together they glistened in the yellow and green light like a living veil.

There are times when the experience of living in this world is rapturous. And there are times when it curls us crying in our beds. Between these extremes we tell one another what we know ...

BURNING HER BRIDGES

Marge was my friend from school. She was married to Mr. Sullivan. They had a big farmhouse with a lot of property, three kids, and his parents living with them. Marge had to do all the work, the cooking, the cleaning, and waiting on the old couple. Finally, she couldn't take it any more. This was in 1959. Walked out of the house one day with nothing but the coat on her back and came here. Said she was sick and tired of being treated like dirt. And she wouldn't go back, not even when her husband came begging, or her kids came crying. Then she met Fred, and that caused a scandal because he was married and had a good job with the railway. Pretty soon Fred left his wife and he and Marge got an apartment in town. But the company Fred worked for didn't like this so they transferred him three hundred miles away. I told her: You go off with Fred and that'll be the last you'll see of your kids. But she went, burning her bridges. And that's where they lived for ten years as man and wife, though they were never legally married.

Marge and Fred presented themselves well, wearing the best clothes. They always dressed up when they went out, even if it was to the grocery store. We visited them once a year though it was a long way to drive. They had a little trailer they'd done up cute. We'd visit in the afternoon then stay in a motel. It made a nice two-day trip. Then Fred died. Had a heart attack one Thursday afternoon on his way to the bank. Dropped dead in the street. And Marge had no one. It was my brother who arranged the funeral. I can still see Marge in her expensive suit and hat draping herself over the coffin and howling: Fred, Fred.

After the funeral Marge had nowhere to go so she came here again. Mother was with me then, eighty-six years old and failing. We were two widows sharing the double bed. Marge took the empty back bedroom. It had the best view in the house—of the garden and the cherry tree in spring.

She had no money that we knew of but she had her beautiful clothes. That's what she spent most of her time doing, washing and ironing her clothes. On a weekday morning she'd turn up for breakfast wearing a Harris tweed suit and chiffon blouse. In the afternoon she'd change into a dress and pearls for a meal of fried meat and potatoes. With Mother and me in house dresses. But no one said anything, didn't ask how long she planned to stay. We let her be the way she was. She was company for us, someone different. We just kept feeding her and washing her sheets once a week and that was that. Pretty soon it was like Marge had become one of the family; everyone stopping by to see Mother and me would now be seeing Marge as well. She lived with us for two years.

Then one day she packed her bags, called a taxi, and left without so much as a good-bye or a thank you. Years later I read her obituary. It didn't even mention she had kids.

MONUMENT

I revisited my childhood home, the one by the beach, the one that figures in all my dreams, the one I always boasted was the same as ever, that it hadn't been painted or torn down or altered in any way, that it looked from the road as it had done all those years ago. Even though it was shabby now with peeling paint, and the long front lawn was weedy, and the cement border on the driveway was crumbling, and the flower beds were empty, and the small rose garden had gone. I could still conjure up the proud feeling I had had about living there with my parents.

For years after they'd sold the house I would drive past and point it out to friends: See, it's still there—like a monument, intact; not lost, not vanished. This fact gave me comfort—and proof that my life wasn't lost or vanishing, either.

Then I became curious to see the inside of the house and whether it also remained unchanged. So after all those years I drove down the broken asphalt driveway. And there was the covered patio where I'd played jacks and tossed my lacrosse ball. And here was the same door handle with the metal worn thin, and the door itself which was a slab of painted wood.

I knocked on the door. A middle-aged woman in exercise wear answered. She told me she was the owner and when I mentioned that I had once lived in the house she invited me inside. Entering the front room I was surprised by a crowd of people: groups of old women sat at tables playing cards and laughing; an old man in baggy pants pushed a walker; more old people sat quietly on chairs.

The room was stuffy, overheated. But through the window at the far end of the room I could see the unchanged beach—the cool stretch of sandbar, the smooth summer sea.

The woman told me the house was a nursing home—that there were ten residents plus activity workers, caregivers and kitchen staff—and that this accounted for the crowding.

My father built this house, I told her.

A lot of people say that, she said, and smiled.

But he did! Look! Here by the front window is the place my mother sat with her knitting and spied on the oriental cleaning woman who lived across the street. She called her Hop Sing; she lived with an older man called Mr. X.; he was bald and drove an oil truck. And here is the place my father sat in his blue recliner before supper to watch the news when he was home, weary from his job on the ships. And that door over there led to my bedroom; it had a three-quarter bed and a dresser painted grey.

We went into this room. It was a kitchen. Two women in white aprons were dishing up the old people's dinner—meat pie and mashed carrots—something I had often eaten as a child, with a glass of milk, my father glancing up from the supper table to the bright sea beyond the kitchen window and saying, I think I'll cut the grass tonight, and my mother saying, it's about time.

I think you'll be happy here, the owner said.

AUTHOR INTERVIEW

1. Thank you.

2. Sure. Appears to be. But isn't.

3. Five of us, actually. Though everyone's left. Except us.

4. School. Work. One to a nursing home.

5. That's right. Two of us in this big house.

6. Not bad. I write. He cycles. We visit the others.

7. Oh, every few weeks.

AFTERWORD

THE CELESTIAL SPHERE

M y father says: I learned to do everything at sea; through the years I did it all. I knew knots and painted decks, and as an officer I handled men. But what I liked best was navigation. The instruments, the calculations. I liked the accuracy and being sure. Before radar we used the stars. I knew every important star in both hemispheres; my calculations were never wrong. I navigated ships under sail and ships using steam and fuel. Through all kinds of seas and on both sides of the equator. I knew the currents in all the oceans. My specialty was manoeuvring around the obstacles—the sudden storms, the change of currents, engine problems, the deadlines for delivering cargo. I could read the sky, the wind, knew rain, clouds, fog, air pressure. I could tell what weather was coming by smelling the air. Even the ocean swells. Standing on deck at night, just by the roll of the ship, I could tell you how high, how fast they were running. All these things went into my navigation. It was more than numbers. It was my life. But it wasn't what I lived for.

From "Navigation," *Word of Mouth*, 1996